"Is it safe to get up?"

He checked the mirrors once more. "Yeah, I think so. I shot one of them. Probably slowing them down. If the ghost was out there, too, then he'll make time to get the drone before following us."

As she sat up, she noticed his arm. His sleeve had a hole and there was blood.

Panic threatened to squeeze the air from her lungs. She forced herself to breathe. "You're bleeding."

"I'm aware. Consequence of being shot."

"We need to pull over. I have to check you."

His gaze bounced up to the rearview mirror. "No." He stomped on the gas, racing through a yellow light that was turning red, and made a hard left onto the main road that led out of town.

BIG SKY SHOWDOWN

JUNO RUSHDAN

To unsung heroes who make the world a better, safer place.

Recycling programs for this product may not exist in your area.

ISBN-13: 978-1-335-69043-2

Big Sky Showdown

Harlequin Enterprises ULC
22 Adelaide St. West, 41st Floor
Toronto, Ontario M5H 4E3, Canada
www.Harlequin.com

HarperCollins Publishers
Macken House, 39/40 Mayor Street Upper,
Dublin 1, D01 C9W8, Ireland
www.HarperCollins.com

Printed in Lithuania

Juno Rushdan is a veteran US Air Force intelligence officer and an award-winning author. Her books are action-packed and fast-paced. Critics from *Kirkus Reviews* and *Library Journal* have called her work "heart-pounding James Bond–ian adventure" that "will captivate lovers of romantic thrillers." For a free book, visit her website: junorushdan.com.

Books by Juno Rushdan

Harlequin Intrigue

Ironside Protection Services

Big Sky Slayer
Big Sky Safe House
Big Sky Showdown

Cowboy State Lawmen: Duty and Honor

Wyoming Mountain Investigation
Wyoming Ranch Justice
Wyoming Undercover Escape
Wyoming Christmas Conspiracy
Wyoming Double Jeopardy
Corralled in Cutthroat Creek

Cowboy State Lawmen

Wyoming Winter Rescue
Wyoming Christmas Stalker
Wyoming Mountain Hostage
Wyoming Mountain Murder
Wyoming Cowboy Undercover
Wyoming Mountain Cold Case

Visit the Author Profile page at Harlequin.com.

CAST OF CHARACTERS

Kimi Redbird Wheeler—After Kimi's brother died on a deployment, she changed her life, leaving the rodeo circuit and becoming a nurse. Despite her best efforts to stay away from trouble, it keeps finding her, nonetheless. She's reluctant to get help from Takoda, a man she's secretly loved for years, but she's left with no choice.

Takoda Yazzie—A former Air Force combat engineer turned private investigator with Ironside Protection Services. He made a promise not to touch his dead best friend's younger sister, but he'll risk everything, including his life, to protect Kimi.

Thomas Wheeler—Kimi's estranged father. He's a renowned geologist and expert in palladium exploration who is missing.

Chance Reyes—A sharp attorney and in charge of the Ironside Protection Services office in Big Sky Country.

Logan Powell—Good friends with Takoda and Kimi, he's also a detective with the Bitterroot Falls Police Department.

Declan Hart—A special agent with the DOJ Division of Criminal Justice.

Ed Macon—Chief of the Bitterroot Falls Police Department.

Chapter One

The days of running headfirst into trouble were over for Kimi Redbird Wheeler. Or so she thought.

She no longer dated bad boys or partied late into the wee hours when nothing good ever happened. Even traded in her rodeo buckles for a nursing degree. No more barrel racing. No more bronc riding. No more taking the risk of breaking her neck.

For the past four years, she tended to the sick and mended the broken.

After her big brother Jacy died, she got her act together. Now, at twenty-nine, she was finally the woman he'd hoped she would grow into. Grounded. Thriving. Doing her best to stay out of harm's way.

Yet, no matter how hard she tried, she simply couldn't steer clear of trouble.

Or rather, trouble was determined to follow her, regardless of what she did.

Kimi glanced over her shoulder. She only saw ordinary pedestrians on the busy Main Street in downtown Bitterroot Falls. *He* wasn't back there.

Nonetheless, she had that feeling again. The eerie prickling sensation skittered across the back of her neck like a colony of fire ants, making her shoulder blades bunch together in reflex.

Someone was watching her. Tracking her.

Kimi quickened her steps, hurrying to The Beanery. The café was the last stop on her list of errands, after hitting the bank, the home goods shop for a new lamp, and the supermarket. The Beanery was the one to-do that was a must-do because she'd been craving a pistachio latte all day on her shift in the emergency room.

Her vintage chambray-blue cowgirl boots that she loved to wear on her time off when she didn't have on sneakers clacked against the cold pavement. She slid a furtive glance across the street.

Nothing. He was nowhere to be seen. Like the slippery shadow dogging her every move was a figment of her imagination. Two or three times she'd questioned her sanity, wondering if it was just in her head, the way he'd appear and vanish.

She rarely got a good glimpse of the man who had trailed her for three days. But her gut told her he was there. Somewhere.

Whipping another quick look over her shoulder, she scanned the faces of the others on the street. Many she recognized as friendly, law-abiding citizens of the small town of Bitterroot Falls. None she knew well enough to call a neighbor or turn to for assistance without sounding paranoid, or worse, hysterical, because…

She still didn't see *him*.

No sign of her shadow.

Not that she had ever seen his face outright from a full-frontal perspective, but she had spotted him enough times to feel confident he wasn't the short man, sixtyish, with glasses perched on the bridge of his nose and an umbrella in his gloved hand, or the tall, thin man who had an aristocratic bearing, wearing a red scarf wrapped tightly around his neck and carrying a brown paper bag filled to the top with groceries.

Kimi and Mr. Red Scarf had checked out of the supermarket around the same time. Now he and Mr. Glasses were close behind her.

In the past several days, she'd tried to ignore the feeling of warning she got every time she caught sight of her shadow. More than once, she'd dismissed it as a byproduct of listening to too many true crime podcasts, blaming it on an overactive imagination. But Jacy had taught her to trust her gut.

She worked in Cutthroat Creek, frequented Bitterroot Falls, and lived in between both quaint, quiet towns where it wasn't odd to see the same faces over and over again. It was to be expected. That was normal.

Which was part of the problem.

Kimi could describe Mr. Glasses and Mr. Red Scarf in detail and, for that matter, most other passersby on the street. Yet, she'd never quite seen the face of her slippery shadow. Too elusive.

Perhaps if she could look the man square in the eyes for a few seconds, without him trying to hide, she might overcome her mounting fear whenever he popped up.

The best description she had was a white male or light-skinned Hispanic. Taller than average. Facial hair. Dressed in plain dark clothing. Sunglasses covered his eyes, day or night. Basically, he looked like a scary thug who intended to rough her up the first chance he got.

Dread curdled in her stomach.

Why would someone want to hurt her?

She didn't have the faintest idea. Even in her wildest rodeo days, she hadn't given anyone a reason to follow her with the intent of bodily harm.

Kimi stopped in front of a flower shop, her palms growing sweaty in spite of the frigid January temperature. Disregarding the gorgeous displays of fresh blooms, she used the glass's reflection to survey her surroundings. At six o'clock in the evening, it was already dark outside, and the winter gloom cast a dreary, sinister pall over everything.

No one was lurking suspiciously. It seemed all clear.

But the prickle along her spine flared again. There was no doubt in her mind that he might be out of sight at the moment, but he wasn't far.

Waiting for the chance to do…what?

An icy chill slithered down her spine as her shoulders hitched.

She moved on from the store, hurrying to catch back up to the two older men, Mr. Glasses and Mr. Red Scarf. The street was busy but not crowded. People were dipping in and out of stores. No one was loitering outside, engaged in conversation. Not in this frosty weather.

Her brother Jacy had taught her what to do in such situations.

Keep calm. Pay attention. Go to where there are people.

In her case, stay within shouting distance of people. Since the elusive guy had started tailing her, she carried her cell phone in her coat pocket as opposed to inside her handbag in the event she needed to call the police quickly. One less step to slow her down.

She increased her pace, bringing her closer to the men in front of her.

The cold air had grown damp, the wind whipping up, like a storm was brewing. One that would bring lots of rain rather than snow. She pulled the hood of her parka up over her head.

Her hold on the plastic handles of her bags began to slip. Adjusting her grip on the groceries, she shrugged the strap of her handbag higher on her shoulder.

Two more blocks and she'd be at the Beanery. One decaf pistachio latte would soon be hers.

"And then head home to cook dinner," she muttered, realizing she'd used her outside voice when a couple passing in the opposite direction gave her a curious glance.

Talking to herself was a quirk that had emerged after Jacy's death. He'd been more than her big brother. He'd been her idol, her best friend in all the world. The one person she fell back on for everything, good or bad. Mostly bad until she'd straightened up, but he had been there to clean up her messes. Her mom, Aiyana Redbird, was an artist, off traveling the world, following her bliss, only checking in now and then. Even less once Jacy was gone. It wasn't unusual for months to go by without hearing from her mother. While her dad, Thomas Wheeler, lived in Bitterroot Falls, and he could see her if he so desired. She was just a simple phone call away, but the only thing he cared about was his work. He lived and breathed palladium mining.

When Jacy died on a deployment with the air force as a combat engineer, she had processed her grief by talking to him. Keeping him alive, in spirit. The habit spilled over during times of high anxiety and turned into speaking to herself more than to Jacy nowadays.

"Yep, I'm going to have a sugary drink before dinner," she said low, this time to her brother. Something the old Kimi would have done without a qualm about spoiling her appetite.

One more block and hello pistachio latte.

She reached the corner, thinking about the warm frothy drink that would delight her taste buds, just a ten-second lapse in focus, and she didn't spot him until it was too late. The shadow lunged from the side street that was little more than a dark, dreary alley.

A gasp tore from her lips with the first hard, jarring yank

of her purse strap on her shoulder. The man jostled her painfully, like she was nothing more than a rag doll. She should've worn the bag across her body.

It wasn't until she had to free her hands to fight back that she fully grasped the gravity of her situation. The plastic bags went flying out of her grip, the groceries tumbling to the ground. The porcelain lamp crashed on the pavement, shattering to pieces.

"Help!" she cried out, holding on to her purse. She struggled to get back onto the busy Main Street, but the man grabbed her by the hood of her coat, hauling her backward, forcing her deeper into the alley.

He was so strong. So much stronger than her.

The second brutal tug on her purse sent her spinning into a wall. Her cheek smacked against the brick, the breath rushing from her lungs. Pain exploded along the side of her face, and that quickly jolted her out of the momentary shock that froze her reflexes.

"Oh, my God!" someone shouted. "She's being mugged!"

Kimi tightened her hold on her leather strap. The man whipped her around, slamming her into the wall. Her skull snapped back against the solid brick. In the daze fogging her brain, she realized that in addition to the usual sunglasses he also wore a ski mask this time.

Her head cleared, and she threw a kick, the chunky heel of her boot connecting with bone or a kneecap.

A loud grunt sputtered from the man, but he didn't stop.

And neither did she. Kimi gripped her purse strap with one hand and punched with the other.

Let it go, Jacy would've told her.

Just give the man what he wanted, her handbag, and this assault might end. The credit cards could be frozen and the cash in her wallet wasn't worth her life.

Let it go.

But she couldn't. She flat-out refused.

This was her only designer handbag, and her twenty-fifth birthday present from Jacy. The Burberry bag matched the vintage boots. Both had been the *last* things he had ever given her.

And then there was the principle of the matter. She might've buckled down in lieu of winning buckles, but she would never give in to anyone, especially not some two-bit street thug.

The bruiser was built like a tank, square and squat and solid. He had his meaty fist locked around her strap. He nearly ripped the handbag from her desperate grip, and would have had to, if not for timely help from others.

Mr. Glasses whacked him with an umbrella while Mr. Red Scarf wielded a red mesh bag of oranges like a weapon, walloping the guy, blow after blow.

"Call the cops!" someone yelled.

Onlookers at the entrance of the alley pulled out their cell phones. Others held them up as if they were recording, with bright lights shining in their direction.

Kimi held tight to the leather strap, but she managed to grab the man's ski mask and yank it down.

Throwing an elbow back into Mr. Red Scarf and shoving Kimi to the side, her assailant lowered his face away from the cameras and disentangled himself from the free-for-all scuffle. The slippery shadow darted down the dark alley, heavy boots thudding on the concrete. He was running fast for a big guy, but he was getting away. The man skirted a dumpster, rounded a corner and disappeared.

People clustered around her and guided her out onto the sidewalk of Main Street.

"Are you hurt?" one person asked. "Are you okay?"

Nodding, she was breathless from the fight and grateful for the heroic assistance of strangers.

Kimi put a hand on the shoulder of one of her saviors, opening her mouth to thank him, and gasped from the sharp pain that radiated in her jaw. She pressed a palm to the side of her face that was throbbing.

The wail of a siren pierced the air, and she sagged with relief.

But she couldn't help wondering if the man who had been following her for three days would try again. Not that she could let it get that far. To the point of another attempt to mug her. To steal her handbag.

As soon as the thought popped up in her mind like a creepy jack-in-the-box—she never understood why anyone would make such a toy—she felt like she was losing her mind again.

Why would someone follow her just to mug her?

She wasn't rich. Sure, the designer bag was beautiful, but it cost less than a thousand dollars. Not worth the effort to trail a person and try to rob them. Unless he was a junkie.

Drug addicts made poor choices. Desperate decisions that were born out of their need to get their next fix. Even if it made little sense.

That had to be the explanation, right?

Mr. Red Scarf handed her a bag of frozen peas. "Here you go. Put that on your face."

"Thank you," she said, taking the chilled bag. She pressed the frozen peas to her cheek and winced. Her head pounded. She was going to have to forego her pistachio latte and go to the hospital. Ten to one, she had a concussion. "To both of you." She glanced between Mr. Glasses and Mr. Red Scarf. "I don't know how I can ever repay you for what you did. You risked so much by jumping in to help me. A stranger."

They could have been hurt and if her attacker had had a weapon, then much worse might have happened.

"Think nothing of it," Glasses said.

Red Scarf nodded. "This is a good town, with good people. Can't stand by and do nothing." He winced and rubbed his head.

"Are you hurt?" Kimi asked.

"He got me good in the face. I think I'll have a shiner in the morning."

She handed the chilled bag back to Red Scarf. "You've already done more than enough. I can't take your peas, too. Not when you need them."

The sirens drew closer. Police and, most likely, an ambulance would be there soon. Then she'd tell them her story. Maybe they would believe her.

Maybe they wouldn't. There was no way they'd give her a hard time about the attempted mugging since she had plenty of witnesses.

It was the part about this being premeditated that worried her. The part where she couldn't accurately describe him. Or his vehicle, other than it was a black SUV. Or how no one else had seen this man following her.

Once, in the hospital parking lot, she'd been talking to her ex-boyfriend, Danny, an ER doctor, and tried to point out her slippery shadow. Before Danny had seen him, the guy had disappeared.

Poof. Gone like he had never been there.

Like he didn't exist.

"Did anyone see his face?" Kimi asked. "Get it on video? A picture?" She couldn't be sure, but she hoped she had pulled down his mask long enough for someone to have captured his face.

The crowd surrounding her murmured as folks looked at

their phones, most likely searching through the photos and footage they had.

"No," one person said, followed by another and another.

Her heart sank.

She knew how this was going to play out. A cop would file a report, tell her to be careful, to be on the lookout for this suspicious man who she couldn't describe and no one else had seen prior to today.

Then she would be left to deal with it on her own.

Unless…

Groaning, Kimi shook her head. "No, I can't go to him."

"Go to who, honey?" a woman asked her, and Kimi realized she had spoken out loud.

"No one." *Just talking to myself again.* Which would only feed into the perception that she was losing it.

Takoda Yazzie would not want to see her, much less help her. The last time they'd run into each other at the hospital—*six weeks and four days ago, and yes, she was counting*—she had asked to speak to him for a minute. Sixty seconds, in private, like two adults. He had stared at her, a muscle ticking in his jaw as her heart stuttered in her chest, waiting for him to respond.

A curt shake of the head. He had grunted and mumbled, *I'm working*, and then couldn't get far enough away from her fast enough. To make things worse, other people they both knew were present, watching and listening. They'd probably thought she had a communicable disease the way Takoda had treated her.

Working. That had been his excuse.

They had been standing in the middle of the emergency room, where she had been wearing scrubs and a nametag because she was working, too.

Sheesh. He wouldn't give her one measly minute.

It had been so humiliating; she had wanted to scream. And not at the universe. Oh, no. She'd wanted to scream at him, in his face, and stab his muscular chest with her finger and give him a piece of her mind.

After that embarrassing encounter, she had vowed then and there that she didn't need him. Not for anything. Didn't even need to speak to him if that was the way he wanted to handle the situation. Seemed immature from her perspective, and she was younger than him by five years.

But she could be just as tough and distant as Takoda if pushed. Even tougher. Colder.

She took a breath, not sure if she was more upset about Tak or the failed mugging.

Go see Tak. The voice in her head sounded so similar to her brother's it made her heart ache.

Jacy would have insisted that Tak, the friend he'd loved like a brother, was the one person she needed to turn to since Jacy wasn't there to help with this latest mess that she found herself in.

"This is a good, clear video," someone said, handing her their phone.

Kimi pressed Play on the recording and watched the horror she had endured play back. The violence that had unfolded so quickly. The brutality that could have ended so much differently if others hadn't selflessly intervened on her behalf.

Her gut clenched and she wanted to retch. "Do you mind if I send myself a copy?"

"No, of course," the woman said.

"Thanks." Kimi texted herself the video file.

What if that big bruiser came back? What if she didn't have the kindness of strangers to save her next time?

As much as she hated the idea and knew she might regret it, doing what her brother would want was better than the alternative.

She needed to see Takoda.

Chapter Two

Gravel crunched as a vehicle pulled up his driveway. Takoda Yazzie set down the pile of mail he needed to open along with his beer on the coffee table and got up from the sofa. He strode to his front window, peeled back the motorized blinds and looked to see who was visiting him at ten o'clock at night.

None of the guys he worked with at Ironside Protection Services had called to say they were stopping by, which they would have done.

Popping up unannounced was considered rude in his circle of friends.

The motion sensor lights on the garage came on, illuminating the sapphire-blue Subaru Forester that parked. Tak recognized the car.

It was Kimi's.

Every muscle in his body went rigid, and he swore. The absolute last person he wanted to see on his doorstep, at night, after he'd been drinking, was Kimimela Anne Redbird Wheeler.

Her full name was a bittersweet mouthful, and the woman was more than a handful. It was easier to wrangle a wild bull than to get her to listen. Or cooperate. Or heed prudent advice.

The only way Jacy had gotten her to settle down and grow up was by dying.

A pang of remorse nearly split him open. Four years since

he'd died. Sometimes the sorrow, the guilt and the shame felt as fresh as that first day when he'd lost his best friend.

He sucked in a breath. Stared out the window.

The Subaru was still running, headlights on. Why was she sitting in her car?

If she was waiting for an engraved invitation to come inside, she'd be waiting forever because he had no intention of letting her set foot across the threshold.

It would be even better if she reconsidered this drop-by altogether, backed out of his driveway and went home. They did not need to do this. Talk about what happened.

He felt bad enough as it was. For his carelessness. For his selfishness. For making the one mistake that he'd promised Jacy he would never make with Kimi.

Tak didn't even know how it had happened.

Well, yes, he did. They were at the snazzy rooftop bar at the BMH—the Bitterroot Mountain Hotel—sitting under a heater, drinking. He drove her home. On the ride, they were talking about Jacy and discovered a strange coincidence. Sometimes they both heard Jacy's voice in their head, maybe out loud. She started crying. Shared grief pricked his eyes and swelled in his throat. He wiped away her tears, his palm caressing her soft, warm skin, his fingers tangling in her silky hair. Then somehow her mouth was on his and they were kissing.

Really kissing. And groping. His hands slipping into places they did not belong. Her hands finding spots that ached for her touch.

Even worse than breaking his promise to Jacy that he would stay away from his baby sister, Tak had almost messed up things for Kimi. She was a nurse, who was sort of dating an ER doctor, the way her brother wanted. Kimi and her boyfriend had taken a little break, but Doc Dan had asked her to move in with him. Despite the break, she was mulling over the idea of living with the doctor.

To Tak, that was the next logical step. The right move for her. Literally. Then an inevitable engagement would follow.

In a moment of weakness, Tak had almost, *almost,* stopped her from becoming Mrs. Doc Dan one day.

He wanted to slap himself silly and not stop until he could forget about the mistake he'd made. The only problem was kissing Kimi Anne was unforgettable.

She was unforgettable.

Her car door finally opened.

Tak stepped away from the window.

Bracing himself, he established some quick ground rules.

Don't let her in. Keep the conversation short. No touching. And definitely no kissing under any circumstances.

Compartmentalization was his strongest skill. He just had to stuff all his messy, complicated feelings about Kimi into a steel box, lock it and bury it.

Simple.

His doorbell rang.

"I've got this," he said to himself.

You had better, a voice replied.

He had to look over his shoulder to be certain Jacy's ghost wasn't standing there behind him.

Sucking in a fortifying breath, he moved away from the window and flicked on the porch light. He steeled his backbone and opened the door.

Kimi had retreated down the steps and was standing off his porch, out of the light in the darkness. As though she was prepared for how this had to go.

Wrapping her arms around herself, she shivered, and he would've liked nothing better than to warm her up. But…

Jacy's sister was off limits, he reminded himself.

Keep your hands and thoughts in check, man. Lay a finger on my baby sister and I'll kill you. Jacy had told him that outright eleven years ago. Tak had met Kimi, and his best friend must've seen the unbridled heat in his eyes whenever he looked at her.

Tak schooled his features. "What are you doing here?" he asked, deadpan, but the words still came out harsher than he'd intended. So he added, "At this time of night."

"I'm sorry to disturb you like this." She lowered her head and shook it. "Maybe I should've called first."

"That would've been polite."

She spun away from him, her flared wool skirt whooshed around her, and she marched off down the walkway. Got about midway. Turned around and stomped back to the foot of his porch. "I didn't call because I didn't think you'd answer and, if you did, I knew you wouldn't let me come over."

"Then you thought right," Tak said, his voice steady, formal.

Huffing a breath, she muttered something too low to completely make out, but he caught his name and a dirty word.

"Are you going to invite me inside?" she asked, grudgingly, like mustering the question had taken a herculean effort. "Let me get out of the cold and get warm in front of your fire?"

Bad idea. The innuendo alone of getting warm by his *fire* made it sound even worse.

Crossing his arms, he stepped out onto the porch. "Why are you here, Kimi? Shouldn't you be snuggled up with Doc Dan or is he working?"

"Tactless Tak strikes again." Kimi sighed. "Thanks for giving me the reception I expected. You could try being a little less predictable."

He gritted his teeth. In business, he was known for his tact. Not only was he a consummate professional, but he'd been raised to handle any unexpected confrontation with a mask of calm control.

With Kimi, things were different. Around her, he tended to forget himself. The way he had the night she had expected him to drop everything and come running to have drinks with her while her boyfriend was working late in the emergency room, busy saving lives. The fool that Tak was, he had, and they had gotten too close, crossing the line. But they hadn't crossed the point of no return. No serious, unfixable damage done. He intended to keep it that way.

"It's cold." He gave her a hard stare. "And I'm waiting."

"I need to talk to you."

"Okay." He shrugged. "So, talk. I'm listening."

Her face was cast in shadows, but he thought he caught the narrowing of her eyes.

"Not out here on your front stoop." She groaned, shaking her head like he was the most obtuse man on the planet. Tactless, thoughtless, as well as discourteous. "I need a friend. Can you be that? Let me in? Let me get warm? Ask me if I'd like a drink? I could sure use one."

That was how the disastrous mistake had played out last time. She'd needed a friend. Wanted to talk, over drinks, about moving in with DD.

This time, he was the one shaking his head. "We've done this dance, kiddo. Fool me once, shame on me. Not happening again."

"Fool you?" She dropped her arms to her sides, hands clenching into fists. "What exactly are you insinuating, Takoda Yazzie?"

Whenever she used his full name, it meant Kimi was getting fired up to light into him. He braced himself.

"That I lured you in?" She sounded aghast. "Tricked you into kissing me?"

"Your words. Not mine. But you did kiss me, and not to offend you, I simply kissed you back."

"What?" Rocking back on her heels, she gaped at him. "That's—that's not how it happened."

"It's how I remember it, kiddo."

"Stop calling me that! I am not a kid," she said, stomping a foot like she was having a tantrum. "I'm almost thirty years old, for crying out loud." She huffed, her breath crystallizing the air.

He was painfully aware that she was no longer a kid. Hadn't been back when they'd first met either. At eighteen, she had been a blossoming young woman.

Now, she was all woman. Filled out with curves guaranteed to wreck him. Black, lustrous long hair and deep brown eyes in a face that was…pure *wow.* And when she smiled, it was like a sucker punch to his soul every time.

But she wasn't smiling now.

"Forget it," she said, waving a dismissive hand in his direction. "I should have my head examined for coming here, thinking that you would help me. Oh yeah, that's right, I already did have my head examined by Danny, who is indeed still working. By the way, I have a concussion. Not that you care. But my brain injury explains my poor judgment in coming here tonight." She spun on her heel and marched down his walkway, heading for her car.

He was off the porch, right behind her, his chest tightening at the mention of her being hurt. "Kimi."

"Look at what you do to me! I came here calm and collected, and you turn me into a raging, unhinged fool. I don't know why Jacy believed you would be there for me. That I could count on you when I needed you the most. He's probably rolling over in his grave with disappointment at how you're letting him down. Letting me down. And if he's not cursing your name, you better believe that I will be," she said, every barb she threw, hitting its mark, straight down to the bone.

"That's a mighty low blow."

"You earned it."

He couldn't disagree.

Kimi opened the car door and hopped in.

Tak grabbed onto the top of the door frame, preventing her from closing it. "Hang on. How did you get a concussion?"

"I won't trouble you with the story or my presence on your property a moment longer." She tried to shut the door.

He held fast to it, moving inside the opening and peering over at her. In the light, the bruises covering half her face were apparent. "Holy hell! What happened to you, kiddo?" He reached for her cheek.

Kimi slapped his hand away. "Don't you dare touch me," she snapped, the look she gave him cutting.

"All right," he said, raising his palm. "Tell me what happened."

"I was mugged. Well, almost. By this big guy. Relatively speaking. You're probably a little bigger."

"Did the cops catch him?"

"No. Witnesses recorded part of the altercation, but his face was covered the entire time. Sunglasses and a ski mask."

"Are you okay?" Leaning closer, he put a hand on her shoulder.

She swatted it from her body. "Don't. After the way you spoke to me just now, after the way you've been treating me, not taking my calls, avoiding me in public—"

"I didn't avoid you when we bumped into each other at the hospital." That was six weeks ago. Way too long, he admitted to himself. But he'd been trying to give her a wide berth, plenty of space to sort things out with her boyfriend and take the leap at moving in. Part of him wondered if she had. Okay, all of him wanted to know if she was shacking up with the doctor. "We talked that day."

"Talked? You uttered two words to me." She held up one finger and then slowly raised a second. "Two, Tak. That's not a conversation, and the way you looked at me, like you wished I would just disappear. I'm not going anywhere, by the way. Do you have any idea how that made me feel?"

Tak needed more than a slap in the face. He needed a punch to the groin. At the hospital, he'd been a bit brusque to keep her from cornering him.

Hurting her so deeply had not been his intention.

As if it wasn't bad enough that he had dishonored his best friend's wish, broken a promise. Keeping that promise, to never act on any romantic urges—physical or emotional—toward Kimi was the least he could've done.

What was wrong with him?

That made him the worst.

At the hospital, he hadn't been running from her—well, maybe he was just a little—but he was so ashamed of himself. Facing her was a terrible reminder of what he'd done.

Not only for kissing her back, but for what had happened on that last deployment. The truth of how Jacy died.

If only he could tell her. But the words were clogged in his throat.

Kimi glared at him. "You think I want to ruin our friendship. But you're the only person I can talk to about Jacy. The only other person who knew what he was really like. Who can tell me things about him that no one else knows. Who still misses him as much as I do." Tears welled in her eyes, but she dashed them away with the backs of her hands, not letting them fall. "The kiss was a drunken mistake. One that we both clearly regret. Friends should be allowed to make mistakes. To talk about it and be forgiven. Have things move forward beyond the awful slip-up. Like mature adults. But I guess you're not capable of that, kiddo!"

This woman knew how to wound and humble him like no other. "I'm sorry. You're right."

She stared at him, mouth open, beautiful brown eyes glassy with unshed tears. "What did you say?"

Clenching his jaw, he drew in a long breath. "You heard me."

"Could you repeat it? Wait a minute." She pulled her phone from her pocket. "I want to record it."

"Get out of the car." He took her arm, urging her from the vehicle, and then closed the door once she was beside him.

Rain started falling, only a drizzle, but the sky would open up soon. Not letting her go, he ushered her up his porch steps and across the threshold.

Now, he had broken every ground rule. Except for one.

Closing the front door, he let her go and vowed to keep his lips to himself tonight. "Can I get you some aspirin?"

She shed her coat, hung it up and collapsed onto the sofa in front of the crackling fire. "I'd prefer a whiskey."

Another bad idea. "Don't you need to take something for the inflammation?"

"Give me some ice and a drink. I deserve it." She gestured to her bruised face, and he wanted to beat the guy who did that to her into a pulp.

Tak got her an ice pack, two fingers of whiskey, and sat beside her. Shoving his mail aside on the table, he grabbed his beer.

He reconsidered their proximity and scooted away a couple of inches.

Staring at him, she shook her head. "What? Do you think I'm going to throw myself at you? That you're so drop-dead hot that I won't be able to control myself?" She arched an eyebrow.

Did she think he was drop-dead hot?

No, of course not. She was being sarcastic. He was aware he generally didn't have problems meeting women, but drop-dead hot?

No way. He also knew he wasn't Kimi's type. She went for extremes. Charismatic bad boys that most women drooled over or boring, passive professionals like DD. Tak was squarely in the middle, in looks and temperament.

"You did say that I have an effect on you," he replied, his tone teasing.

Kimi slapped his arm and scooted closer to him. "You have a bad effect on me. Raging. Unhinged. Remember?" She put the ice pack on her cheek. "Not melting in a puddle of desire at your feet. Get over yourself."

He was in no danger of getting an inflated ego. "Tell me what happened," he said. "Start at the beginning. Don't leave anything out."

"Three days ago, I was leaving work and noticed this guy sitting in the parking lot."

"Make and model of the car?"

Shrugging, she sipped the whiskey. "Black SUV. Big. Like a Chevy Tahoe or GMC Yukon. Maybe a Ford Explorer. I don't know. I'm not good with cars."

American make, which was a start. "Same guy who attacked you today?"

"Yes."

"How can you be sure? You told me his face was covered the entire time. Sunglasses and a ski mask."

"I'm sure," she snapped. "Okay? He wasn't wearing a ski mask in the hospital parking lot or any other time I've spotted him. Just sunglasses. Tonight, when he attacked me, he wore a ski mask for the first time. But I managed to yank it down for a moment. It's the same guy."

Deciding to let it go, he nodded and took a draw on his beer. "Okay."

"Anyway, he followed me into Bitterroot Falls."

"And you didn't notice the make of the vehicle behind you?"

"It was dark, all right, and he wasn't close enough. He always keeps his distance."

"But you're sure it was him following you?"

She sighed. "I picked up tacos for dinner and when I was headed back to my car, I spotted him on the street, looking in the window of a store two doors down. Stuff like that kept happening. I'd catch a glimpse of him here and there and then he was gone."

"For the past three days?" he asked, skeptical about the length of time, but she nodded. "Did you point him out to anyone? Notify the cops?"

"Danny and I were talking in the parking lot one night at the hospital. I noticed the guy. Tried to show him. But the man took off before Danny saw him. As far as calling the cops, I didn't know what to say without sounding hysterical or paranoid."

"You didn't see his face tonight because it was covered. In all the times that he's followed you, have you gotten a good look at him? Not a single picture of his face?"

She narrowed her eyes like he was the enemy. "No, but I'm not making this up. This guy has been like a shadow. Appearing and disappearing. Sticking to me even when I try to lose him. I'm sure that the same guy who has been following me attacked me tonight. I'm certain of it."

"You said he almost mugged you. Did he just go after your purse?" This made no sense. Why would a petty thief interested in mugging a woman and snatching her purse follow her three days? "Did he say anything to you?"

"Not a word. After he dragged me into an alley, it all happened so fast. You can see for yourself. Someone captured part of it on video and shared it with me." She took out her phone, brought up the footage and hit Play.

Watching the video, seeing this guy hit Kimi as she struggled to hold on to that silly bag, and then as others stepped in to fend off her assailant, filled his veins with ice. He didn't even realize he had been holding his breath until the video ended and he handed the phone back.

Irrational as it was, he felt that he should have been at her side, protecting her.

He wasn't her boyfriend and couldn't be with her in the way that he wanted.

But he could keep her safe. If she followed his instructions.

"Thankfully," she said, "some people heard the commotion and came to help me."

He wanted to raise his beer in a toast to Good Samaritans. "Next time, you let a thief take your handbag, your wallet, your jewelry. Better than him taking your life."

"Jacy bought me this purse." She patted the handbag she wore crossbody. "I know it wasn't smart, but I couldn't let him take it."

Looking down at the soft blue-gray bag, Tak remembered Jacy had given it to her for her twenty-fifth birthday, along with the boots she had on now. Jacy had purchased them separately, but the boots and purse had matched, and her brother knew she would love them. So did Tak. Watching her light up after she opened the box was one of his top favorite memories.

Second only to kissing her.

Compartmentalize, man.

"I don't want there to be a next time. That's why I came to you," she said. "Help me figure out what's going on."

Tak frowned. As upsetting and disturbing as her story was, there wasn't much he could do. Maybe he could tail her, see if this shadow turned up again. He had a ton of vacation days that he needed to take and even if he didn't, Chance Reyes, his boss and friend, would give him the time off.

"Listen, I don't want you to go home tonight." He had installed a state-of-the-art security system at her house with help from some of the guys at IPS, Bo and Eli. Bitterroot Falls and Cutthroat Creek were quiet towns, but as specialists with Ironside Protection Services, they handled all sorts of security, investigative and intelligence solutions. One thing they didn't do was take unnecessary chances, especially not with family and friends. They'd hooked her up with surveillance cameras, motion sensor lights and an alarm. The firewall protected her Wi-Fi and smart locks from hackers. A standard set up for themselves and all those in their circle. They'd even installed a generator to ensure everything continued to run during a wicked winter storm that might knock out the power. Still, it was best to act on the safe side. "Unless home is now with Doc Dan," he said, fishing to find out if she was living with her boyfriend.

She stared at him, not saying anything, her eyes growing hard and narrowing to slits. By the twitch of her lips, something unpleasant was simmering beneath her self-possessed surface.

"Until I can figure this out, I don't want you to be on your own. Stay with DD," he said, using the nickname she hated for the doctor.

Lowering her head, she set her glass down on the table with a clink. She dropped the ice pack beside it. "Turn to

Danny and rely on him. That's your answer?" She stood and strode to the door.

He trailed behind her, perplexed by why the suggestion would rankle her. Doc Dan was her boyfriend. Staying with him, the same way she had done many nights beforehand, was a sensible idea.

"I don't want you to go home alone right now," he said. "You have floodlights, but there are still pockets of darkness where someone could hide and wait for you to come home." The image of some masked man springing out of the dark, wrapping an arm around her throat and hauling her inside to do only goodness knew what made his heart clench. "I don't know why this guy would go to the trouble if he only wanted your purse. You probably won't see him again, but you should take extra precautions for the next few days while I look into it. Okay?"

Kimi grabbed her coat and put it on. "Yeah, sure."

"Hey." He put a hand on her shoulder, turning her around to face him. "I need you to listen to me and do as I say, for once. Go stay with your lucky boyfriend. Play house with the doctor for a few days. Try it on, see how it feels." It might assuage some of her doubts about taking the next step with the ER doctor and she might realize there was nothing to fear. Doc Dan was established, had a lucrative job, was nice; more importantly, he treated her well—all the things Jacy had wanted for Kimi. Things Tak wanted for her, too. Every happiness with a man who deserved her. "Give me time to sort it out. Make sure you're not in any danger."

She stood at attention, heels clicking together, and gave him a mock salute. "Yes, sir."

Swearing in his head, he knew she wasn't going to listen. "Don't 'sir' me. I work for a living." It was a military thing. Having been enlisted once, he did not want to be confused for someone in the privileged position of an officer who delegated the real work.

"Good night, Tak." She was out the door, her hood pulled up over her head, and running in the rain.

He watched Kimi climb into her car and drive away, his gut hollow with foreboding, his mind roiling with the images from the video of her attack.

Swearing, he grabbed his keys and his coat, then hustled to his car in the downpour. He'd follow her to make sure no one else was.

First thing in the morning, he'd get to work figuring out who was after her and ensure the guy stayed away. His one responsibility to Kimi was to keep her safe.

Chapter Three

Standing at the nurses' station, Kimi lifted her head from the medical chart she was writing on and spotted Dan. He was headed in her direction, his gaze locked on her.

She had done her best to dodge the conversation they were about to have for the majority of her shift. Not that she'd had to try very hard. A nasty six-car pileup on the interstate had packed the emergency room, filling every medical bay. The staff had been hustling for the past four hours.

Things tended to be relatively slow in comparison to today. Cutthroat Creek Community Hospital served folks in the town it was named after, the people who worked at the nearby oil field, and handled overflow from Bitterroot Valley. Plenty of nurses were always available, but they were short on doctors. Hence the reason Danny often pulled extra shifts.

The ER hadn't been this busy since the mass shooting in October. Both Bitterroot Falls and Cutthroat Creek had been rocked to their foundations. During the investigation, the number of casualties had reached an alarming new high. Not only civilians but SWAT team members as well had been treated. The DOJ Division of Criminal Investigation had worked with Ironside Protection Services to apprehend the sniper. Everyone at IPS had become a local celebrity overnight.

Making it impossible not to think about Tak after the incident in his truck, where he had kissed her, not the other way around even though she had welcomed it.

Now Takoda wouldn't talk to her, but he was everywhere. News articles. Featured in magazines. Hosted on podcasts. Doing charity work in the community, something IPS did often. She was forced to see his devilishly handsome face and not be able to talk to him.

Not even when he was on her turf in the emergency room.

"You shouldn't be at work," Danny said, putting a forearm on the desk and leaning toward her. He wore green scrubs that matched his eyes and well-worn sneakers. "You should be resting."

Setting down the chart, she looked over at him and a little pang of regret niggled in her chest. Not for ending their relationship. Regret gnawed at her over the fact she had let things continue for as long as she had, knowing, deep down, that she didn't love him. "It's only a mild concussion. I'm fine to work."

Danny stared at her with an intense look. "I'm the doctor and I disagree." He rubbed her arm, flashing one of his best bedside smiles.

If only she felt hot and bothered, yearning for more when he touched her the way she did whenever Tak's hand was on her, things might've been different.

"I thought you'd go to my place last night," he said. "After I discharged you, that was the agreement. You stay with me so after my shift I could monitor you, wake you every couple of hours, or you had to be admitted."

"If I stayed on your couch, you wouldn't have gotten any sleep. Which you need to function." She dug in her pocket and fished out the house key he'd given her once he finished examining her and put it in his hand.

The chatter at the nurses' station had stopped and they had a captive, not-so-discreet audience.

She touched his elbow and guided him away from the desk, toward an alcove with a water fountain, safely out of the earshot of the other nurses who were eager for a chance to be with him. "I can't be at your place."

"Sure, you can." He cupped her cheek. "I want to be there for you. We're still friends."

"You don't look at me like a friend." Not any more than she looked at Tak as a friend or a substitute big brother.

Affection for her radiated in Danny's eyes. He was sweet and nice and loyal. Good-looking, too. He was everything she should have wanted.

"I'm sorry I'm not more present and that work dominates my life, but I realize I could've made more of an effort." He sighed. "I'm even willing to go to the next powwow with you."

Willing. Like he was doing her a favor and she should be lucky. "We're not a good fit, Danny. It's no one's fault. We just don't click."

"Since we broke up, I haven't been able to stop thinking about you. I miss you, Kimi."

The difficult thing was, she knew that he was truly sorry. For all their missed dates. For how he was constantly tired. For not wanting to go to the Crow Fair Celebration, the largest Native American event in Montana, the biggest powwow in the country. For showing no interest in half her culture. For how everything in his life, his job, his mother, playing golf when the weather was nice, all came ahead of her.

On their first date, he'd been upfront about his vigorous work schedule, which she had witnessed firsthand. He'd claimed he'd had a midlife epiphany on his forty-first birthday and was determined to make changes. Starting with her. That he was ready to settle down.

After four months of quasi dating, things never felt right between them. The desire to make Jacy proud by settling down with a nice, stable guy, her need for intimacy, for an emotional and physical connection, had made her stick it out long past the relationship's expiration date. She'd realized she wasn't settling down, simply settling, and called it quits with him. But Dan had suggested not making it final, taking a break instead. Then, as what she could only assume was a knee-jerk reaction, he'd asked her to move in with him. To consider it, like it was a solution. When she'd talked things over with Tak at that rooftop bar, it dawned on her that Danny didn't need *her.* He wanted someone pretty and flexible, who would squeeze into his life, causing as little disruption as possible.

And that was definitely not her.

Kimi removed his hand from her face and held it. "I care about you and I'm glad you care about me, too. But our time together is done." She gave his fingers a small squeeze before letting him go.

His remorseful expression disappeared, replaced by cool professionalism. "I'm sorry you feel that way. I was hoping you would change your mind. Spare me from going through this dating process all over again with someone new."

The one thing Danny was not—a romantic.

"You've been kind not to rush into dating another nurse. I appreciate it." Even though the real reason apparently was that he had hoped to avoid the hassle. "But you should get back out there. Madison would be a good match for you." The perfect, pretty Lego block. Kimi predicted they'd be married in a year.

Danny gazed at her for a long moment. "Have you gotten back out there? Is that the reason why you didn't come over?"

"No, it isn't. I'm not dating anybody, and I slept alone."

His frown deepened, as though he was skeptical. "I thought you would've gone to Takoda," he said, studying her face. "Had him look after you."

She had confessed to Danny about the kiss with Tak, one all-too-brief kiss, and didn't use alcohol as an excuse. Even though they'd been on a break, they hadn't agreed to see other people. Ashamed of herself for violating his trust, she'd apologized profusely.

Danny had acted relieved that she hadn't slept with Takoda. Hadn't appeared fazed about a kiss. To her, that kiss was still a betrayal. Maybe because it had meant something to her. A whole lot more than any kiss with Danny ever had.

So, she had ended things, for good.

"I don't need anyone to look after me," she said. "What am I, seven? I don't need, nor do I want, a babysitter. I stayed at the hotel. The BMH is pretty nice. Had the front desk call me every three hours and gave them instructions that if I didn't answer, to have someone on staff enter the room and check on me."

"Good. I'm glad you're taking your concussion, which is not mild, seriously." He put a gentle hand on her arm. "We needed you earlier with the victims of the car crash. Things have calmed down. Get out of here. I don't want to see you back in this ER for at least forty-eight hours unless you need treatment for some reason. Doctor's orders. Understand?"

She nodded. "Okay. I'll get out of here."

He patted her arm, and she went to the locker room.

The only time she left the hospital in her scrubs was when she was too exhausted to change or in a rush. Taking advantage of an empty dressing room, she opened her locker and took her time changing into the extra outfit she kept at work. Jeans and a V-neck sweater. She released her hair from the topknot and finger-combed the strands. After swapping her running shoes for her favorite cowgirl boots from Jacy, she threw on her coat and made sure to wear the strap of her handbag across her body. Putting on her leather gloves, she headed out into the brisk night air.

She hurried toward her vehicle, scanning the parking lot for her shadow. Just when she thought it was all clear, a man emerged from a gunmetal-gray truck parked nearby, making her pulse spike. Someone she hadn't been expecting.

Takoda.

The guy had the most irritating habit of materializing out of nowhere. A quality that her slippery shadow shared. She'd have to circle back around to that coincidence.

Wearing a silverbelly Stetson, he strode toward her, his cowboy swagger dialed high, making her breath catch in her throat. He reached her car first and leaned against her door, all six-foot-three of him, hard, honed muscle, blocking her from getting inside. Tipping her head slightly back, she stared at him. His golden-brown complexion and sharp, chiseled features reflected his mixed heritage of African American and one quarter Navajo. His thick black hair was cropped short, and his dark brown eyes were piercing.

The man was one tempting package.

Well, some naive women might find him tempting. After twenty minutes in his presence, they would discover that there was nothing tempting about Takoda Yazzie. Except for his devilishly handsome face.

And his sinfully hot body.

Kimi remembered what it was like to be held in those strong arms, pressed tight against all that warm, solid muscle. She shivered, and not from the frigid breeze.

Just forget about it. Forget about him. She wasn't sure if that was her voice or her brother's.

Not that it mattered. Wanting something, or rather someone, she couldn't have, was an exercise in futility.

Silence hung between them in the bitter cold.

"Well, what are you doing here?" she asked, not in the mood for a staring contest. "You made it clear last night that you weren't going to help me."

"Not true. You don't listen to me, kiddo."

Kimi bristled.

Every time that Tak opened his mouth, he had all the charm and personality of a cantankerous wolverine. Even more off-putting, he never stopped letting her know that he wasn't the least bit interested in her as a woman.

Calling her *kiddo* was a stark reminder of how he saw her.

Kimi folded her arms. "I may not do as you say, but trust me, I listen to every single word that leaves your mouth." Her gaze dipped to his full lips, and to her shame, she ached to kiss him.

"Then you would've heard me when I told you I'd look into it and handle things if you were in any danger."

Her pulse was still thrumming. His unexpected presence outside the hospital flustered her. And when she got flustered, she got snippy. "You ordered me to run to Dan and let him protect me."

Tak had a way of bulldozing people, but she was just as good at standing her ground.

"I'm not here to fight," he said. "We need to talk about a couple of things."

"Not out here." When he didn't budge, she said, "Move." She shooed him aside and, surprisingly, he pushed off her car and stepped out of her way.

She climbed into her Subaru, let the engine warm up, and pulled off. He was in his truck not far behind her.

Now that she had an escort, she could go home in the dark and grab some things without worrying about being ambushed and attacked a second time.

Her house actually belonged to her mother. Kimi had been entrusted with taking care of the place while her mom gallivanted, free of responsibility. Living as she pleased. Loving who she wanted. Having fun. Nurturing her passion. Odd how that had once been Kimi, doing the exact same thing on the rodeo circuit. It was like she'd swapped places with her mother.

Oh goodness, she had turned into Aiyana Redbird. Who had also once been a nurse. How much Mom had changed—really, they both had—after Jacy died.

For the better.

Strangely, Kimi was happier than she had been before. She liked the routine with less risk. Helping people during challenging situations came with its own reward.

Jacy had been right about a lot.

But not everything.

It was nice, putting down roots, serving her community and building friendships. Though all her friends were also Takoda's. Bo Lennox, Eli Easton, Chance Reyes and Autumn Stratton from IPS, along with the rest of the Stratton *season sisters*: Winter, who was in love and living with Chance, and Summer as well as her fiancé, Logan Powell. During Kimi's frosty standoff with Tak, he'd staked claim to all of them.

Maybe their absence from her life was more striking after her breakup with Danny. No one had excluded her from anything. She still received the invitations to their group dinners, the Sunday funday brunches, Logan and Summer's engagement party, and the holiday parties. But she hadn't wanted to endure a repeat of the hospital run-in with Tactless Tak. So, she'd made excuses and gone into self-imposed isolation.

It sucked.

Kimi turned down her road and pulled into her driveway. The floodlights above the garage remained dark. They were motion-activated and should have popped on.

She got out and by the time she closed her car door, Tak was beside her.

"Did you adjust the settings on the lights?" he asked.

"No. I figured there might be a short circuit."

"I thought you'd be spending the night at the hotel again."

She stiffened. "How do you know that's where I was last night?"

His mouth tightened. "How do you think? I followed you because I knew that you wouldn't listen. Why didn't you go to DD's?"

Kimi rolled her eyes. "Stop calling him that." She went around the car and started up the walkway. "I didn't because we broke up. A while ago."

He took hold of her arm, stopping her, and a quiver spread over her as it always did when he touched her. "You should have told me you two weren't together anymore."

"What would've been the point in telling you? Hmm…" she said, and he looked down at her. "Would you have offered to let me bunk with you instead?"

Something flashed in his eyes for a second, a spark that brightened his impassive dark gaze. Then whatever it was disappeared as quickly as it had appeared, making her wonder if she'd truly seen anything at all.

Don't delude yourself, she decided. If that hint of heat had been real, that would mean she ignited some emotion in him other than irritation. Not that Tak, her brother's best friend, wanted her.

Wolverines were solitary creatures. Some never even mated.

Although he had been the one to initiate the kiss that night in his truck, he hadn't done it out of desire. He had kissed her out of pity. Plain and simple.

She'd been crying and he hadn't known how to handle her tears. He'd felt sorry for her. Kissed her to make the crying stop. And it worked. End of the pathetic story.

"Well?" she demanded when he just stood there staring at her. "What difference would it have made? You don't care."

His expression remained a stony blank mask, but the muscle along his jaw twitched. "I care." He cut his gaze from her and glanced around. "None of your security lights are working."

She looked up at the house. The lights around the front of the perimeter hadn't come on either. "Do you think they're all on the same circuit board?"

"Get back in your car," he said, his voice lowered. "Drive to Mr. Simpson's house and wait for me there."

Kimi tensed. Mr. Simpson was her closest neighbor, the only one within shouting distance out there on the outskirts of Cutthroat Creek, where the houses were acres apart. "Why?" she asked, matching his hushed tone. "What's going on?"

"I don't think there's a short in the circuit." Drawing a gun from inside his coat, he nudged her toward the driveway. "If you see or hear anything suspicious, take off and go to IPS. A couple of the guys are still at the office."

Something inside her went stone-cold. "What about you?"

"I'm going inside to look around. Make sure it's safe."

"We should stay together and call the police." She curled her hand around his forearm. "Let the cops search the house."

He shook his head. "What if it's nothing?"

"What if it's something?" she countered.

Tak frowned. "Call 9-1-1 on your way to IPS." He dislodged her clenched fingers from his arm and nudged her again, prodding her to move away from him and toward her car. "Listen for once, will you." His voice was a rumbling whisper. "Go."

He stood there, eyes narrowed, waiting for her to leave.

Kimi stifled the groan rising in her throat, then hurried to her Subaru, jumped behind the wheel and did as he asked. Only because Mr. Simpson lived across the road. Kimi backed into her neighbor's driveway, stopped beside his truck and cut off the lights but kept the engine running. She hoped Mr. Simpson didn't come outside to ask why Kimi was sitting there. At least his dog, Bandit, hadn't started barking yet, alerting him to her presence.

With a clear view of her own house, Kimi watched Tak tread up the steps to the front door. He tried the knob. The door must have been locked, which was a good sign. He started entering the digital code on the keypad to get in. She knew the code for his place as well.

To be used in case of emergencies only.

When he wasn't speaking to her, she had contemplated letting herself into his house. Imagined sitting on his sofa, waiting for him to get home to confront him. Then that fantasy somehow morphed, and she was naked, waiting to kiss him.

So, she'd abandoned the entire idea. A pity kiss was one thing.

Pity sex?

No, thank you. She did *not* want that. Not even if it was with the sexiest man she'd ever met.

Takoda crept into her house, shutting the door behind him. Maybe she should call the police now, to be on the safe side. It could take them ten to fifteen minutes to get there.

Movement from an upstairs window drew her gaze. The

curtain in the guest bedroom slid to the side, and her breath stalled in her lungs. A figure peered through the glass. There was someone else in the house. Whoever it was, they wore a ski mask. In the moonlight, it seemed as though their head canted in the direction where Tak's truck was parked in the driveway.

Did Tak know he wasn't in there alone?

The curtains in the bedroom drew closed.

Panic welled in her chest. She clenched her hands on the steering wheel, not sure what she was going to do.

But she had to do something.

And fast.

Chapter Four

With heightened caution, Tak closed the door quietly and crept deeper inside the house. He reached out for the wall, feeling around for the light switch. Found it. Flicked it up. Nothing.

The place was dark. And cold. All the power had been cut. That meant the generator had been tampered with, too.

He pulled back the curtains in the front room. Moonlight illuminated a shocking sight. Kimi's living room was in a shambles. He moved through the house quickly, but with care not to step on anything that would make noise. Furniture had been turned over. Cushions ripped and torn apart. Delicate items that had once held sentimental value were shattered. Bookshelves emptied and dumped on the carpet. Someone had also busted in the drywall, making huge holes, as though they were looking for something they thought Kimi had. It might explain why, possibly, that same person had tried to snatch her purse.

A cold draft drew his attention toward the other end of the house.

The kitchen had been tossed as well. Cabinets opened. Drawers yanked out. Food and dishes and utensils thrown on the floor. He noticed the back door that led to the small, gated yard was slightly ajar. The wood on the casing near the strike plate was broken. Like someone had kicked the door in. He turned the light from his phone into the darkness outside and glanced around. No one was lurking in the yard and the gate was open. Perhaps whoever had been there had left.

He made his way back through the ransacked house.

Once Kimi saw this mess, she was going to have a conniption. That was fine by him. Her anger he could handle. She used it like armor, hiding other emotions. Hurt, mostly. And sometimes, fear.

She never liked to admit when she was either. Better to be angry and stubborn.

Why was it so easy for him to see through her?

He didn't want to, but it had always been that way. Even when she had acted like an invincible wild thing out on the rodeo circuit. He'd seen it for a lie, a different kind of armor that masked insecurities and doubts and fears.

Tak saw clearly who she was—a complex, beautiful woman who didn't want anyone else to see her vulnerability.

A woman so determined to honor her brother's memory that she'd overhauled her entire life. Went back to college. Became a registered nurse.

A woman he aimed to protect.

With the first floor clear, he headed to the carpeted stairs. Each step he took was steady and soft and silent. He listened on his way up.

No sound of any other movement.

Although it had been a while, Tak had been in the house many times and remembered some of the floorboards upstairs creaked. Reaching the landing, he took a wide step at the top to avoid one plank that squeaked.

Stilling, he paused for a moment. There was no noise from anyone rifling around upstairs.

Maybe the house was empty.

He figured he would start with the first guest room and

work his way down the hall. He eased into the bedroom doorway. The curtains were pulled closed, only a sliver of moonlight from the window slicing the darkness.

Taking another step deeper into the room, he noticed it wasn't in disarray like downstairs. Not tossed and searched. It was possible whoever it was had lost steam by the time they'd reached the second floor. Or they hadn't had a chance to search *yet*.

A floorboard groaned beneath shifting weight. Too late, he realized that someone must've been concealed behind the armoire.

He spun in a defensive move, deflecting the blow intended for him. Operating on training and instinct, Tak threw out an arm and snatched the weapon before his attacker had a chance to strike again. It was something long and solid, like a pole. He tugged it hard, trying to knock his assailant off balance. But another blow came from behind him, striking the back of his head.

Pain blasted in his skull, flaring down to his jaw and into his neck. Tak dropped to a knee, fighting to stay conscious. But he kept hold of both his gun and the weapon he had wrangled away from the other man.

There were two attackers in the room with him. Not one.

Loud barking erupted just outside the house.

Tak took advantage of the noisy distraction and swung the pole or stick, striking a leg.

A man swore, but the two assailants made off into the hall.

Harsh whispers, male voices.

"We're running out of time to find it."

"Let's go."

Hurried footsteps pounded on the steps.

Downstairs, the front door banged open, wood slamming against the wall. The distinctive sound of a shotgun cocking, a shell pumping into the chamber. Ferocious barking grew louder, closer, from the entryway.

"Bandit!" Mr. Simpson said, calling his German shepherd. "Sic 'em, boy!"

Panicked footsteps scurried toward the back door. A man cried out. Something clattered to the floor, breaking. A door slammed.

Then a shotgun blast cracked the air.

Tak staggered to his feet, smothering a wave of nausea. He needed to get to Kimi.

An engine roared, a heavy rumble—a full-size pickup truck, Tak guessed—and tires peeled off with a squeal.

He moved quickly into the hall and onto the stairs.

A bright light shone in his eyes and he raised an arm to block it. His face tingled. Spots danced in his vision. His head ached.

"Takoda!" The light lowered. Kimi ran to him, meeting him in the middle of the staircase, and threw her arms around him in a tight hug. "Are you all right?"

"Yeah. I'm fine." He was a bit woozy, not what he would classify as *all right*, but his only priority was getting her to safety and keeping her out of harm's way.

Not letting him go, Kimi kept an arm around his waist as they went the rest of the way down the steps. In the light from the flashlight she carried, he got a good look at the weapon the man had tried to use against him before he'd managed to snatch it. Adorned with genuine leather and hand-beaded craftwork, fur and prayer feathers, it was a Native American walking stick. The crowning feature was a hand-carved bear on the top. It belonged to Aiyana.

Mr. Simpson was in the hallway, crouching down, petting his dog, who was standing on all fours, alert and wagging its tail.

"Is Bandit okay?" Tak asked, hoping the dog hadn't been injured fending off the intruders.

"You betcha. He managed to take a chunk out of one of those burglars. The guy almost shot him, but I opened fire, and the sound of my shotgun made them hightail it out of here." Mr. Simpson patted the dog and stood up, cradling the shotgun in his arm. "This boy is built like a tank. Aren't you, Bandit?"

The German shepherd gave a high-pitched bark that sounded like he agreed.

"Thanks for hurrying over," Tak said.

"Sure thing. Kimi told me there was a problem. That's what neighbors are for. You need me to stick around? Give a statement to the police?"

"You can go home. If the cops have any questions for you, they'll swing by." Tak shook the older man's hand. "Everything you did is much appreciated."

"Good to see you, Takoda. I wish it was under better circumstances. You should come around more often and keep this one company." He pointed a finger at Kimi. "So she doesn't have to be in this house alone all the time. What if she had come home by herself with those two robbers in here? I shudder to think what could've happened to her."

Anger took hold of him at that thought, and Tak nodded. Immediately, he regretted it, pain spreading into his teeth, hammering behind his eyes. Pain he'd accept if it meant Kimi was safe. He wasn't going to give anyone the chance to hurt her.

"This is usually such a quiet, safe town. Heck, I still leave my keys in my car and my front door unlocked. I can't believe someone broke in," Mr. Simpson said. "Probably drug addicts would be my guess. The meth epidemic has spread everywhere. Come on, Bandit." The neighbor left with his attack dog.

Tak rubbed his forehead. The sharp pain in his head was settling into a persistent, pounding throb, but he tried to ignore it.

He turned to Kimi. "I told you to go straight to IPS if there was any trouble. This proves you don't listen."

"I heard you. I just choose to follow my mind rather than your orders after I realized there was someone in the house with you. By the way, you're welcome. But I didn't know there were two of them." Kimi stepped toward the living room and gasped. "Oh, my God. First, I almost got mugged and now my house has been turned upside down. At least the cops won't be able to dismiss this as some random act of violence."

They'd call the police, just not right now. She didn't need to stare at the wreckage of her home for hours while the police did their job. Besides, the longer they stayed there, the more time whoever had broken in would have to strategize while they were aware of Kimi's whereabouts. They might decide to circle back, park, wait for them to leave and follow.

No way in hell Tak was giving them that opportunity. "I want you to pack a bag."

She pivoted toward him. "I have two days of stuff in an overnight bag at the hotel."

"That's not enough. You need to pack for at least a week."

"Why?"

"Come on." Not answering her question, which would only inspire more, he took her by the arm and led her upstairs into her bedroom. The priority was getting her out of the house. Then they could talk. There were still two things he needed to tell her, and it was going to lead to difficult discussion.

Kimi grabbed a bag and gathered some of her things.

He caught the smell of honeysuckle. Vivid, sun-kissed radiance. Easy to recognize since it was Kimi's favorite scent. It was the top note in her perfume and maybe even her shampoo since it kicked up whenever she ran her fingers through the long hair that she always wore loose and free unless she was working. The smell grounded him, helping him shake off the pain, but it also made him laser-focused on Kimi.

Her hourglass silhouette. The way she moved. The intensity she put into everything she did.

How close she came to danger.

"Why do I need so much stuff?" she asked, closing a dresser drawer.

"Because you're not coming back here until we get to the bottom of what's going on. And I'm not sure how long that'll take."

KIMI STOPPED PACKING and stared at Takoda. He wasn't telling her everything.

Something was wrong, besides the fact that two men had broken into her house and torn it apart for some reason. She could hear it in his voice.

He wasn't simply short-tempered and frustrated with her for not following his instructions earlier. There was an edge. A strain in his tone. Worry, not just irritation, and…*pain*?

She set her bag down. Getting closer, she shone the light on him. He squinted and turned his head away. She looked him over. Spotted a suspicious dark patch on his head. She touched along his hairline, behind his ear. He sucked in a sharp breath.

Definitely pain.

Her fingers came away wet with red. "You're bleeding and you've got a nasty lump. You are not fine. We should go to the hospital and have you examined."

"I'll be fine once I get you out of here."

Shaking her head in disbelief, she went to the adjoining bathroom and washed her hands. "Come in here and sit down. I'm not leaving until I clean you up." She needed to be sure the wound wasn't serious.

Huffing a breath, he marched into the bathroom, lowered the lid of the toilet seat and sat while she pulled out a medical kit from the cabinet.

"It's nothing," he said, "really."

"I'll be the judge of that." Slipping in between his spread legs and standing in front of him, she shone the light in his eyes, and he shuttered them reflexively. "Stop squinting," she ordered. "Your pupils aren't dilated, which is good." She aimed the flashlight at the injured spot on his head. Leaning in to see better, she brought her chest close to his face, and he went rigid. She soaked some gauze in saline solution and used it to wipe away the blood.

He flinched with a hiss and clutched his knees.

"Sorry," she said, not meaning to hurt him.

"The sting surprised me."

He had a one-inch-long gash. Not terribly deep. "Provided the bleeding stops, you won't need stitches. But you might have a concussion."

"Probably. But it can't be fixed by going to the hospital."

True.

She propped her knuckle under his chin, tipping his head up. "Any blurred vision?"

"No."

"Weakness or tingling in your arms or legs?"

"No."

"Severe neck pain?" She slid her hand over his cheek and down the side of his neck. "Or how about any nausea?"

His eyes locked on hers in the dim light, and the air between them stirred, charged with electricity.

She wondered which was worse, being attracted to this hunky man or pretending she wasn't?

Maybe if she told him how she felt about him. That she'd loved him since she was eighteen years old when he'd strode into the kitchen and looked at her, turning the power of his smile her way. If she admitted her feelings, he'd probably reject her, but then she might be able to finally move on without wanting him. "Takoda—"

"I'm fine. Are you finished packing?" He set his hands on her waist, setting off a flurry of nerves in her belly, and then he shuffled her backward, out of his way. "We're leaving. Now."

He was up and out of the bathroom before she could process what had just happened.

"What's the big rush?" She put the medical kit away, gathered extra toiletries, and went to her bag in the bedroom.

"One of the things I wanted to tell you was that I followed you today. There was no one else watching you. He, or they, probably figured you'd be at work for your entire shift. So, they were here, searching your house. But you left the hospital early."

She swallowed around the sudden lump in her throat. "What on earth do they want from me?"

"That brings me to the second thing, but I don't want to get into it here. Let's go." He took her bag from her hand, and they headed down the stairs.

"What about calling the police? Don't I need to file a report?"

"I'll call Logan and ask him to handle it," Tak said.

Logan was a detective with the Bitterroot Falls Police Department. Technically, she'd met Logan first, before Takoda had. Kimi had gotten to know the cop and his fiancée last year during a murder investigation that had brought them both to Big Sky Country. The two had ended up moving to Bitterroot Falls. Since Logan and Chance were best friends, it was through Tak and her association with IPS that Kimi had gotten to know the detective and the season sisters better.

Kimi had been invited to Logan and Summer's engagement party close to Christmas, but decided to skip it, dreading the cold bite of another public rejection from Tak. Consequently, she'd spent the holidays alone. The mistake she'd made with Tak, giving in to a reckless impulse and kissing him, had cost her far more than it had him.

Even though the kiss had been mutual. Pity on his side and desire on hers, but they were equally responsible.

They stepped outside the house and he shut the door.

"I guess it's a good thing I still have my room at the hotel," she said.

"You can't stay there. We'll swing by so you can pick up your stuff." He took her arm, his head on a swivel, steering her to his truck. "That guy, your shadow, and his friend searched your place, looking for something. If they didn't find it, they might decide to ask you point-blank about whatever it is."

The image of being cornered and questioned with a gun to her head flashed through her mind. She was not eager to have that scenario play out.

"The hotel isn't safe," he added. "Any idea how easy it is to break into one of those rooms?"

"No."

"Too easy. He could pretend to be hotel staff, delivering room service, a maintenance guy, someone from the front desk dropping off a package. All else fails, he just has to swipe a universal keycard from a housekeeper."

Not one iota of anything he'd just spouted out did a thing to steady her jittery nerves. It only amplified her anxiety.

Tak opened the passenger door for her.

"What about my car?"

"Leave it at Mr. Simpson's. You're going to ride with me."

She climbed into the truck. "But if I can't stay at the hotel, where am I supposed to go?"

"My place."

Did she hear him correctly? "Your place."

He frowned. "Yes."

She stared at him. "I thought you didn't want us getting cozy anymore."

His gaze darkened slightly, then grew strangely blank. "Listen, Kimi. There will be house rules. You'll sleep in a guest room. If we're in a common space, we'll wear appropriate clothing. At the very least pajamas. There will be no getting cozy. Or getting warm by any fires together. No fires at all. Got it?"

Stunned, speechless, she nodded.

His tone softened just slightly. "For Jacy. Okay?"

She nodded again, and he shut her door, hurried around the front end and jumped in the truck.

"Are you okay to drive?"

"I wouldn't endanger you by being behind the wheel if I wasn't." He pulled out of her driveway. "Please, stop worrying about me."

That edge was still there.

"Yeah, okay." But that was easier said than done.

Their first stop was the Bitterroot Mountain Hotel, where it took less than five minutes for her to grab her things and check out. Tak never left her side. Even though the men who had violated the sanctity of her home hadn't made an appearance, she was grateful not to be on her own.

They headed to Tak's house. He had purchased a property that was only a fifteen-minute drive from everything.

Bitterroot Falls. Cutthroat Creek. The IPS office. The Redbird house.

In a haze, she stared out the window, trying to process what was happening. Not the least of which was that she was going to bunk—*correction*, sleep—in Tak's guestroom.

They reached his house. He whisked her out of the truck and ushered her inside. Trudging off down the hall, he dumped her bag in the guest room.

She noted it was the one farthest from his. At least he was letting her stay with him. That alone was an accomplishment. She'd take the win.

Taking off her coat, she let the gravity of things settle in. She plunked down onto the sofa and stared at the cold fireplace.

"Were you serious when you said there wouldn't be a fire?" she asked, rubbing her arms with an exaggerated shiver.

He blew out a heavy breath, strode to the hearth, and built a fire. Once it was going, he sat in one of the leather chairs, facing her. "Happy?"

Not even close. "Thank you."

Now she wanted a drink to chase away the chill flowing inside her, but she wasn't going to push it. Provided she adhered to the rules, there shouldn't be any problems.

Had she packed pajamas?

"Do you have any idea what they were looking for in my house?" she asked.

"No. I was going to ask you the same thing, but that reminds me." He got up, took a folded manila envelope from his inside coat pocket and handed it to her. "That was in my mail yesterday."

She glanced at the return address. There was none, and it was postmarked Monday, two days ago. She peeked inside.

Disbelief rocked through her. She reached in, taking out

a bundle of cash. Large bills with a rubber band around the stack.

Holding the wad of money, she stared at him.

"It's ten thousand dollars," he said.

She reeled back. That was an awful lot of money. "Who sends that kind of cash in the mail?"

"There's a note. Look at it. I need to call Logan."

Turning the envelope upside down, she shook it. A slip of paper fell into her lap, and she read it.

Takoda,

I'm hiring you. To ensure you take the job, I've included a retainer for your services. I've gotten myself into a bit of trouble and may have dragged Kimi Anne into it. If anything happens to me, your job is to protect my baby girl.

I lost one child. Another shouldn't go before their time, especially not because of me.

Thomas Wheeler

A chill raked over her flesh—the sting as sharp as frostbite. She read the note two more times.

Tak was still on the phone with Logan.

Kimi took her cell phone from her handbag and tried calling her father. The line rang six times and went to voicemail. She hung up.

On the rare occasions when they did reach out to each other, it wasn't unusual for either of them to leave a message first before deciding to return the call.

But this was different. With someone following her, mugging her, breaking into the house, the note and money sent to Takoda, this was all seriously bad. And her father was the only one with answers. Surely, her dad expected her to contact him.

Why wasn't he picking up?

Tak slipped his phone in his pocket and sat in the chair, facing her. "Logan is going to check out your house, speak to Mr. Simpson, and come over to get our statements. I'll tell him everything when he gets here."

"I don't understand." She held up the note.

"Neither do I. So, I went to ask your dad while you were at work. No one has seen him in the past four days. Not since Saturday."

Her mouth grew so dry so fast it was difficult for her to swallow. "What are you saying?"

Takoda hesitated, and she wished he would just spit it out. "It appears your father is missing. Whatever your dad was wrapped up in is most likely linked to the shadow who has been following you and the two men who tossed your place. Somehow, your dad has put you in danger."

Chapter Five

As Tak roused in his bed, a ray of sunlight from the window hit him in the face, and it was like a hot needle in his eye. He'd designed and built his house to have the bedrooms facing east with breathtaking views of the mountains and stunning sunrises. The blinds on the floor-to-ceiling windows were automated to lower at dusk and rise at dawn. Right now, he was cursing those decisions.

Groaning, he managed to sit up and make it to his en suite bathroom with no sign of nausea. That was good.

A hot shower helped put him back solidly on his feet. He pulled on boxer briefs, pants and socks. Shrugging on a flannel shirt, he left it unbuttoned as another bolt of pain stabbed his eyes. Thankfully, it faded fast.

Heading to the walk-in closet, he threw on his shoulder holster and secured his weapon inside. The Heckler & Koch Mark 23 was his favorite handgun. A preferred choice in the spec ops community. In the air force, when he was stationed at Malmstrom Air Force Base, assigned to the elite RED HORSE Unit—a highly mobile, civil engineering, quick response force—he'd supported contingency operations and worked closely with Special Forces in austere and hostile environments around the world. Difficulty and danger came with each mission. They were airborne—jump qualified—and had vigorous combat training.

Even though they hadn't had a tier-one designator, they'd had to be ready to handle their own under fire, especially *if* things went south and hit the proverbial fan.

Not if, *when*.

Jacy slid into his mind, but Tak didn't have the bandwidth for grief and guilt. Not this morning.

Inside his closet, he entered the code on the digital keypad of the built-in safe and then pressed his thumb to the biometric fingerprint scanner, a dual-layered security feature. The door popped open, and he scanned his collection of tactical knives that were lined up by size. He decided on his MAMU fixed-blade. From slicing and chopping, to piercing and splitting, the knife's ergonomics were top-notch. Also, it had been a gift from his cousin, Aiden Yazzie, who was a US marshal. They'd grown up together in the Navajo Nation, close as brothers after Tak's parents were killed in a car crash. He'd been so little, lucky to survive, but he didn't remember them. His only living relatives were on the reservation, a sovereign territory roughly the size of West Virginia. They shared stories of his parents, particularly of his father. He hadn't been back home in years, not since his aunt, Aiden's mother, had passed away.

Tak slipped the blade in its sheath and clipped it on his waist. Turning to the shelf with his guns, he picked the Ruger LCP Max. A lightweight, micro-compact weapon that was a powerful backup option at close range despite its small size. He strapped on an ankle holster, tucked the Ruger in, and pulled on boots. Before he closed the safe, he grabbed extra loaded magazines.

Thomas Wheeler had opened Pandora's box, and Tak wanted enough firepower to fight a small war if necessary. He hoped it wouldn't come down to that. Experience had taught him it was better to have a mini arsenal and not need it than to need it and not have it.

He left his room.

The scent of baked goodness hit him in the hall. He made it to the kitchen without another lance of pain.

Kimi glanced up from her spot on a stool at the island, looking right at home in his kitchen. She wore a T-shirt and yoga pants that hugged her legs. Staring at him, she raked a hand through her hair and smiled.

Sucker punch straight to his soul.

"Good morning," she said. "How's your head?"

Kimi had knocked on his door a couple of times throughout the night, waking him to check on him. Thankfully, she'd stayed in the hall and his verbal response was sufficient.

"Better." Still, he went to the cabinet, found the aspirin, and swallowed two pills dry.

"Let me see." She patted the stool beside her.

He'd rather skip letting her get close enough to examine his head again. "No need." Averting his gaze from her, he glanced around. She'd made coffee. A plate of blueberry muffins was on the counter. She'd been busy. "I didn't realize I had any muffin mix in the pantry." He took a mug from the cupboard and poured himself coffee.

"You didn't. But muffins are easy. Basic ingredients. Flour, baking powder, sugar, eggs, butter, salt, milk. I threw in some blueberries from the freezer and added the zest of a lemon. Voila." She spun off the stool and sauntered over to him with the sexy grace of a dancer, her full breasts swaying against the cotton T-shirt.

A bolt of desire pierced him and he struggled to ignore it.

She looped her arm around his and led him to one of the stools. Putting her hands on his shoulders, she forced him to sit, bringing them eye level.

He set his mug on the counter.

She pushed his legs apart, sliding between his thighs, and he stiffened. A hint of a smile danced on her lips. "Turn your head and look down."

He did. His gaze landed on the soft outline of her breast. Her silky hair brushed his cheek, and a hint of honeysuckle invaded his senses. It was all too much. He ached to touch her, to let go of his guilt and his shame and the promises he never should've made. For just a day, for an hour, for ten minutes—even though it would feel like torture. He would take any amount of time where he could stake claim to this woman.

She was so sensual and sweet, so right and yet so wrong for him.

Clenching his hands, he shifted his focus to the kitchen countertop. The cold, hard, flat slab of quartz. Tak needed to nip this—*whatever this was*—in the bud. If only he knew how.

"No more bleeding." Kimi's fingers were warm and gentle as she examined his head, and his throat tightened. "The lump has gone down, and it's only a cut now."

"One more scar."

Her fingers traced his earlobe and she pressed her palm to his cheek. He glanced at her face, skin bare, with no makeup to conceal her bruises—*still, so beautiful.* She was looking down at his chest. She pushed back one side of his open shirt and ran her other hand over a spot that was tight and shiny, where he had taken a piece of shrapnel. Her touch was hot as a brand on his skin.

"I like your scars." Her voice was a husky whisper, curling up his spine, seeping in like smoke. "You got most of them in the air force, didn't you?"

His throat tightened another notch. "Yeah."

"You and Jacy made it possible for others to do their jobs.

For missions to succeed. For wars to be fought and won. Scars are a part of being an unsung hero."

She had no idea. Not one clue.

If she knew the truth—that Jacy's death was his fault—would she still consider him a hero?

She met his eyes, her lips inches from his mouth. "If you smiled more, worked on being less crabby and a bit more charming, you'd be a chick magnet."

"I don't want to be a magnet for women, or anything else for that matter."

She tilted her head, eyeing him like he was a jigsaw puzzle she wanted to piece together. "Not even luck?"

"Luck comes in two varieties." Good and bad. "I'd have to take both, kiddo." At the nickname, she flinched.

He knew it bothered her, but it was the best way for him to remind himself to behave.

"Most men would love to know how to draw women to them," she said, not backing off.

"I'm not most men."

"And I'm not a kid." She slid a palm up his chest. Her fingers danced over his collarbone and brushed across the nape of his neck.

His heart raced while other parts of him hardened. Twelve years of pretending like she was nothing more to him than his best friend's kid sister hadn't done a thing to dampen his desire for her.

Keeping one hand on his neck, she ran the other slowly over his thigh and looked up at him, meeting his gaze.

Blistering need hit him like a bolt of lightning. His restraint frayed. He shook his head, but he didn't move away. "Kimi."

"I know. You're not attracted to me." She dropped her forehead to his. "You probably wish I had never come to you asking for help. Wished my dad hadn't sent a retainer, forcing you to take me on as a job. I know you're only doing this, protecting me and trying to find out what's happening, because you feel obligated."

Is that what she thought? That he wasn't attracted to her? That she was an obligation to him?

If the choice was between him and anyone else on earth protecting her, he'd want her to come to him first, every time. And not because of professional duty or a personal sense of responsibility.

He'd hurt her before by letting her believe something that wasn't true. Letting her think it was easy for him to keep his distance from her. Easy to be near her and not talk to her, touch her. Easy to send her to Doc Dan when it killed him inside because he wanted her right there with him.

Never again would he let her think such things were the truth when it couldn't be further from it.

He longed to kiss her, knowing he shouldn't, but it was going to be the only thing on his mind until he burned it out of his system.

KIMI STOOD BETWEEN his legs, not meeting his eyes, determined to keep her hands on him until he inevitably pushed her away. She braced herself, mustering the strength to tell him how she felt. To throw all her cards on the table, leaving no regrets, on her part.

But then his strong arms wrapped around her waist, his hold on her loose at first. She was too shocked to move, to speak. He slid his hand to her lower back and drew her so close that the gap between their bodies disappeared. So close, the tension could only be relieved by shifting even closer. She pressed her breasts against his hard chest, her pelvis to his, and to her surprise she discovered he was attracted to her.

Heat thrummed off him, and her body responded with a flush of intense awareness.

"I'm always here for you," he said, his voice deep and low, his minty breath tickling her lips. "No matter what. Because I choose to be. Because I want… I want you to be safe and happy."

"How am I supposed to believe that after the way you turned your back on me?"

His callused fingers cupped her chin, tilting her face up. That piercing gaze locked with hers, sending a shiver through her. "Believe this."

Takoda leaned in and she did, too, drawn by a gravitational pull into his orbit, and it was like déjà vu when they met in the middle. Except this time, no tears. His warm lips brushed over hers, tentative and gentle, teasing, almost flirting before he penetrated the seam of her mouth. She welcomed his tongue, savoring the taste of him, lost in the shocking relief of *his* kiss.

The fear, and the worries, and the rest of the world simply faded away. Sliding her fingers around the back of his neck, she arched against him. He tasted so good, felt so warm and solid. His fingers slipped into her hair and his arm tightened around her as though he didn't want to ever let go.

Flutters in her belly went wild. He changed the angle of his mouth, taking it deeper still. Hot and possessive, like he wanted to claim her. She held on to him, relishing the sweet ache of her insides jump-starting since the last time he'd kissed her. A small, needy sound escaped her, and he pulled her in even tighter. That ache coiled through her all the way down to her toes.

The kiss went on and on until she wanted to yank off his shirt. Wanted to pull hers over her head and toss it to the floor.

No regrets. She reached for his belt and unfastened the buckle.

A groan rose in his throat. Gripping her hands, he leaned away, breaking the kiss, leaving her breathless and wanting so much more. "This can't happen."

A cold slap of disappointment hit her, sobering her quickly. He wanted her and she was offering everything, but he… "Why?"

He scooted his stool backward, the legs scraping against the hardwood floor, turned away from her and hopped off. Going around to the other side of the counter, he fastened his belt.

Kimi straightened, staring at him, waiting for an answer. She understood the guys on the rodeo circuit. It had taken a while with Dan, but she'd figured him out and what made him tick. But Takoda was still a puzzle. One she was determined to solve. "Are you seeing someone?"

Keeping any reaction tightly under control, he stared at her. "You should get dressed. We're supposed to meet Logan at your dad's house in less than an hour."

A reminder of her father and the threats to her life was not what she wanted at the moment. "First, answer my question."

"What does it matter?"

The answer was obvious. To her, anyway.

Thank goodness she hadn't made herself any more vulnerable by telling him how she felt about him. Now he was asking ridiculous questions to push her away.

Maybe she needed to push back. "You know everything about my life. About me. It matters. I think it's only fair."

"Oh, hell," he muttered. "I'm not seeing anyone, Kimi. Okay?"

No girlfriend. That was a good start. "The last woman you brought around was Brooke, right?"

"Yep."

Brooke, the waitress. She had dark hair that fell to her waist and bright green eyes, but she hadn't held his interest for long.

"That was what, last year, late summer or early fall?" she asked, casually, as though she couldn't quite remember.

It was mid-September. Takoda had brought her for drinks with the group on the twelfth, and she had been there with Dan.

He nodded. "Yeah."

"Been a while. No one else during the holidays when you were avoiding me?"

Tak sighed. "No."

Then this should've been easy, but for some reason he was making it impossible.

"Surprising for a guy like you." She didn't say anything else, letting the bait dangle, hoping he'd bite.

He picked up his coffee, sipped it slowly. His gaze locked on her. His jaw clenched. "A guy like what exactly?" he asked, unable to resist.

She grinned. "One with needs, who runs through women faster than wildfire through dry brush."

Averting her gaze, he scrubbed a hand over his jaw and rolled his shoulders as though he were now the one who was uncomfortable. "If I have an itch, I scratch it. Plenty of ways to do that without getting entangled in a relationship. Satisfied?"

"Not by a long shot." She drew in a deep, fortifying breath. "Why not me?"

Kimi had seen him in plenty of relationships and was even aware of several of his one-night stands. She wanted her chance with him, but he didn't seem interested in her, like she was defective.

"I promised Jacy. Agreed you were off-limits."

That burst the bubble of her anger. She had a big tumbleweed of feelings for Takoda caught inside her, trying to sort out whether she was in love with him, and he'd promised her brother that he'd never be with her? "When?"

Please, please don't let it be right before he died.

"When isn't the point. He made me swear and I did. Don't ask me to break my word."

Something akin to pain filled her chest. She folded her arms, hoping to stifle it. "I don't believe Jacy would still expect you to keep that promise. Not if what you truly want is for me to be safe and happy."

"I guess we'll never know since he's not here to tell us for himself. This isn't easy for me, you need to know that, but… There's a line with you, Kimi, and I can't cross it."

Chapter Six

As Kimi stormed out of the kitchen, Takoda turned his back, refusing to watch her leave. Emotions he did *not* want to feel swamped him. Filling him. Flooding him. He could barely breathe.

That kiss. He could still taste her, despite trying to wash it away with coffee. And the way she'd felt in his arms, pressed against him. So right. Like they might fit together.

Belonged together.

But he had overstepped, way, way across the line. Now he had to figure out how to pull back.

Tak picked up a muffin and devoured it. Then he ate another. He was ravenous. The only problem was, he wasn't hungry for food.

Cleaning up the crumbs from the counter, he shoved inappropriate thoughts of making love to Kimi from his mind and forced himself to focus on the very pressing problem involving Thomas Wheeler.

Last night, Tak had updated Logan on what had been happening. His buddy had checked out Kimi's house and got a statement from the neighbor, Simpson. Today, they were going to meet at Wheeler's place. See if they could get to the bottom of things together.

Kimi returned to the kitchen fully dressed. But her expression was somber and all traces of passion and humor were gone. "I'm ready to go," she said without looking at him.

They left the house and got in his truck. Yesterday's precipitation had become steady snowfall this morning. He had to turn on the wipers to see the road.

"The muffins were good," he said. It looked as though she'd made a dozen but hadn't had any herself. "Thanks for baking."

She stared out the window. "Sure."

"Did you eat anything?"

"No. I'm not hungry. Only had some coffee."

They had ended things on a sour note, which was enough to ruin her appetite, but she'd had time to eat before he'd entered the kitchen. "Thinking about your dad?"

She nodded. "Yeah. I tried not to for a little while, but then you reminded me about meeting Logan."

The subject of her father was never a simple or easy one. Her feelings about him must have been all over, and Tak didn't want to reopen old wounds. They couldn't avoid talking about Thomas Wheeler forever, but they also didn't have to do it right that second either.

He switched on the radio.

A Morgan Wallen song came on, and Kimi sang along low to "I'm The Problem."

Tak's thoughts circled back to the mess Thomas had dragged Kimi into. One man following her and trying to snatch her purse was bad, but two of them in her house was serious trouble.

"We interrupt normal programming with an emergency bulletin," a radio announcer said. "Radar indicates a polar vortex moving in. A significant winter storm is expected to impact much of Montana and the entire northwestern region starting tomorrow in the late afternoon. Snowfall will range from four to potentially over ten inches in some areas. High winds causing the wind chill factor to plunge well below zero is expected."

Winters in Montana could be rough. Most of the time the snow started falling in September and stuck around through May. A fluctuation in temperatures was an understatement. It was not unheard of to have a forty-degree day followed by one that was subzero. Storms and arctic fronts were common, as were backup generators and four-wheel drives. But a polar vortex could be nasty.

Preparation could mean the difference between living and dying.

They arrived at her father's house early. Since there was no city traffic to deal with, Tak could get to most places in Cutthroat Creek and Bitterroot Falls quickly.

Tak parked in front of the one-story rambler that was situated on a large plot.

Logan wasn't there yet. Last night, the detective had sent a couple of officers, who were out on patrol in Bitterroot Falls, to Thomas Wheeler's, but he hadn't been at home or didn't answer.

Tak and Kimi got out of his truck and headed up the walkway.

Tufts of dense clouds drifted across the gray, midmorning sky, obscuring the sun. A drop in temperature from the incoming storm could already be felt. He zipped his fleece-lined leather bomber jacket against the frigid wind. Kimi wore sensible pants stuffed into fur-trimmed waterproof boots, gloves and the heavy-duty anorak she sported every winter.

Climbing the steps to the front door, Tak held out his hand and Kimi gave him the spare key she had. He pounded on the door a few times—as he had done yesterday when he was trying to track down her dad to ask about the note and retainer fee—and waited. No response.

He inserted the key and unlocked the door.

"Mr. Wheeler?" Tak stepped inside, with Kimi following behind him. "Are you here?"

Leaving the small entryway, he walked down the narrow hall and stopped in front of the living room. Kimi came up alongside him and covered her mouth with a hand.

The house had been ransacked, the same as hers. Torn cushions. Knocked-over furniture. Papers strewn across the floor. There were also the same holes in the drywall. Someone had been determined to find something.

In the light of day, the damage was devastating. Nothing was salvageable. Even the television set had been smashed.

Treading carefully into the living room, he pulled a pair of latex gloves from his jacket pocket. "Don't touch anything," he said to Kimi, and she nodded as she followed him.

A mucked-up crime scene ruined cases. Once, he'd been on an investigation where a rookie cop had contaminated evidence to the point that almost nothing was of any use to forensics, much less being able to stand up in court. After that, Tak made it a habit to always have a pair of gloves on him.

He searched the place, looking for any signs of foul play.

Someone had broken the windowpane in the back door. Glass shards covered the kitchen floor in front of the door.

"When I was here yesterday, looking for your dad, I didn't take the time to check out the back of the house." He'd been worried about leaving Kimi alone at the hospital for too long.

He had called the nurses' station to see if she was working a shift and had been told that she was, *unexpectedly*. There was always the possibility she might not have felt well enough to stay and would've left early. If that happened, Tak wanted to be there to ensure her safety.

"I'm going to check the bedrooms," she said.

Tak followed Kimi down the hall. In all three rooms, the beds had been flipped onto their sides, mattresses sliced open, and wardrobes emptied.

A door closed toward the front of the house. Footsteps approached. *Two people.*

They were only expecting Logan.

Shoving Kimi behind him, Tak drew his gun.

"Takoda! Kimi!" Logan called.

Who was with him? "We're back here," Tak said.

Logan met them in her father's room. He was quick to give Kimi a hug. Another man entered. A uniformed officer from the Bigfork Reservation Police Department. "This is Lieutenant Joe Midthunder. He reached out to my department last night. Someone on the reservation filed a missing person's report for Thomas Wheeler two days ago. Joe hoped Thomas would show up, but then he missed something important yesterday. Something he never would've missed. I filled Joe in and invited him to join us today."

Kimi narrowed her eyes. "Who filed the report two days ago?"

"I'm afraid that's confidential," the lieutenant said. "The person would like to remain anonymous."

"Anonymous?" Kimi folded her arms. "What if they had something to do with the reason my father's missing? What if they have important information?"

The lieutenant shook his head. "They don't."

"Can you at least tell us what Thomas missed yesterday that was so important?" Takoda asked.

"I can't." The lieutenant shook his head. "It's confidential."

"Hold on." Logan raised a palm. "Before you hit him with the same list of questions I already asked, you're not going to learn anything besides the association between your dad and this individual who filed the report was personal in nature and not business-related."

Stiffening, Kimi breathed in, her jaw set hard. She didn't like this any more than Tak did, but he needed to get things back on track.

"There's a Midthunder with the Bitterroot Falls PD," Tak said casually.

"That's my daughter." The lieutenant hooked his thumbs on his utility belt. "She didn't want to work on the reservation." He swallowed hard. "With me."

Difficult relationships between dads and daughters was a theme today.

Logan cleared his throat and turned to Kimi. "Hey. How are you holding up?"

"Fine. I just wish I had some answers." She slid a glance at Lieutenant Midthunder.

"Understandable," Logan said and then turned to Tak. "How's your head?"

"Much better."

"Did you two find anything in this mess?" the lieutenant asked.

Tak shook his head. "We really haven't had a chance to properly search the place. I figured it was better to see if there were any signs of foul play and then wait for you."

"Once you give the okay, Logan, I'd like to look through his things," Kimi said. "See if anything he normally had on him or was fond of is here."

"Sure." Logan nodded. "You'll have to wait for forensics to dust for prints and then still wear gloves."

She nodded.

"Anything in particular you're looking for?" Lieutenant Midthunder asked.

"Um, well." Kimi thought about it. "He wears a signet

ring on his right pinky finger that has the Wheeler family crest on it."

Her dad's side of the family was originally from England and could trace their roots back to the 1600s. The ring was supposed to pass to Jacy after Thomas died.

"His Zamberlan work boots," Kimi added, "and his notebook. Brown leather with strap wraps engraved with his initials. None of those things he'd willingly leave behind. So, I'm hoping if they're not here, then it means they're with him, wherever he is, and maybe he's all right."

"When was the last time you saw your father?" Logan asked.

"At Christmas. I was surprised he called me and invited me to lunch."

Strange. Thomas rarely called her. Never asked to see her. Not even during the holidays. Takoda should've been there for her, to talk it over, see how she was doing. Especially then. After Jacy died, they'd spent every Christmas Eve together, watching movies and cooking dinner before they exchanged gifts. It was one of the best nights of the year for him. He always looked forward to having her all to himself, even though he couldn't have her in the way he wanted, making it also one of the worst nights. To be so close to her while keeping himself at a distance.

Last year, he'd been all alone, thinking she was cozied up with DD.

If only he'd known. He would've swallowed his pride and gone to her.

Thoughts of that kiss threatened to derail his focus, but he blocked it from his mind.

"What did you talk about with your dad when you saw him?" Logan asked.

"Not much. Work. Mostly about his. He was leaving CCMC."

Thomas had worked for Cutthroat Creek Mining Company forever. They were the largest palladium mining company in the region. "Did he say why?" Tak asked.

"Only that he had gotten a lucrative offer from the Stracke Group. TSG deals in precious metals and was looking to open a mine in the area."

Lieutenant Midthunder watched Kimi intensely, like he thought she might be a suspect.

Another strange thing for Takoda to add to the list.

Logan took out his pad and a pen and jotted down notes. "Are you sure his leaving didn't have anything to do with the recent layoffs at CCMC?"

Kimi shoved her hands in her pockets. "He spoke for twenty minutes about how palladium was going to surge in demand and its price was about to skyrocket because congress was going to pass some bill to ban the import of certain minerals from the Russian Federation, specifically palladium. He went on and on about how he was finally going to cash in as the head of the exploration department for the Stracke Group. Twenty minutes of him talking nonstop about that before he even bothered to ask me how I was doing." She flicked a glance at the lieutenant before lowering her head. "Not that he really wanted the answer. He never mentioned the layoffs."

"Forgive my ignorance," Logan said, propping a fist on his hip, "but what's so special about palladium?"

"It's a shiny, silvery-white metal," Tak said, "that's an essential component in the automotive industry, used in catalytic converters. Also in electronics, dentistry and jewelry. I only know so much about it because I got stuck talking with Thomas once."

"After Jacy's funeral." Kimi looked at Takoda and grief

filled her eyes. "Even then, Dad talked more about himself and his own life than his son's."

It might have been the selfishness in Thomas Wheeler, but Takoda always had the impression that the man didn't know what to say in awkward or difficult situations. So he'd fall back on something familiar he was more at ease discussing to fill up the quiet spaces in conversation.

"Did Thomas ever go looking for palladium on the reservation's land?" Tak wondered.

Midthunder shrugged. "Wouldn't have mattered. Thomas knew the tribal council would never agree to selling any rights or building a mine. We respect the land."

"Was he out there at Bigfork a lot?" Kimi asked.

"Depends on your definition of *a lot*, I suppose." Midthunder gave away nothing in his expression. "He had friends out there."

"Were you one of them?" Kimi asked. "Did you know my father well?"

The officer pursed his lips. "I knew him well enough to recognize that, as of yesterday, I should take the missing person's report seriously."

Tak glanced at Kimi. He was certain the same question running through his mind was going through hers. What was so special about yesterday?

"Was that it?" Logan asked Kimi. "Your father didn't say anything else to you?"

"Why did he want to meet in the first place?" Midthunder added.

"To wish me a Merry Christmas and to give me a gift."

Tak moved closer to her. "What was it?"

"A rare first-print edition of *The Wizard of Oz*. He used to read it to me and Jacy when we were kids. He also gave me a necklace with a colorful butterfly etched on the pendant.

When I didn't show any excitement over it, he went so far as to take it out of the box and made a big deal of putting it on me."

In Sioux, Kimimela meant *little butterfly*. But in Algonquin, Kimi meant *secret*. Takoda had only ever heard Thomas call her Kimi. Maybe it was nothing. Maybe it was everything. "Sounds sweet of your dad. Sentimental."

Kimi arched an eyebrow, like the comment had sounded delusional. "My father isn't sweet or sentimental. He's smart. Shrewd. A gifted geologist and mining engineer, and the best surveyor able to find palladium where others didn't think it would be. He's many things, but sentimental isn't one of them."

Midthunder nodded in agreement.

Tak wished he could hold Kimi, but he settled for putting a hand on her arm.

She jerked her arm free of his touch.

Midthunder noticed but remained deadpan.

Also giving him a questioning look, Logan furrowed his brow at the interaction between him and Kimi.

Takoda shook his head at his buddy, a silent plea for him not to ask about it. The tension with Kimi was his fault. "Maybe your father gave you the necklace as a way of extending an olive branch." Deep down, he wanted that to be true, for Kimi's sake, but he doubted that was the reason. The timing of Kimi being in danger and her dad giving her that gift, when he hadn't bought her a Christmas present since she was fourteen, couldn't be a coincidence. "I'd like to see it." He hadn't seen her wearing it the past couple of days.

Maybe the necklace was at her house. The guys who had broken in hadn't gotten a chance to search upstairs.

"Good luck with that," she said. "Every time I looked at the necklace, it brought up a lot of conflicting feelings. I didn't want to throw it away and I didn't want to keep it either. So, I sent it to my mother. Figured she might actually wear it."

Aiyana had the necklace.

Tak groaned. "Is she still living with her companion in Spokane?" Aiyana detested the words *boyfriend* and *girlfriend.* She believed no one past the age of thirty should use such terms to define their relationships. It didn't sound mature or dignified.

Kimi nodded. "Yup. This guy seems to be sticking around."

More like Aiyana was the one choosing to do the sticking. From the stories Tak had heard, after the divorce, Aiyana hadn't been interested in being tied down again. Maybe it was really about finding the right person. "But you kept the book?" Tak asked.

"The necklace made me angry, to be honest. But I found having the book comforting. I guess because it was a reminder that my dad didn't forget about all the things we did together years ago. When I packed to stay at the hotel, I threw it in the bag for some reason. I started rereading one of the stories. Getting mugged dredged up a lot of old stuff for me."

That meant the book was at Takoda's house. They had one of the gifts Thomas had given her and maybe one clue that would get them closer to keeping Kimi safe.

"See if your mom will send the necklace to you," Logan suggested, "express mail."

"I shouldn't have to drag her into this." Her tone was defiant. Angry. Kimi took out her cell phone and started dialing. "I'm going to try my father again. How dare he put me in this predicament," she said, and Tak couldn't agree more.

She put the phone up to her ear.

The four of them stood silently waiting for the call to connect.

Ringing came from inside the room. Thomas's phone was

there at the house. They all looked around, trying to pinpoint its exact location.

Takoda tracked the sound to a corner, coming from beneath a wardrobe. Lieutenant Midthunder helped him shove the two-door wardrobe to the side. The ringing stopped as the call went to voicemail, but the phone was there.

Kneeling, Tak pressed on floorboards. One gave way with a click as he pushed in. Then the board popped up half of an inch. He lifted it.

Inside the cubbyhole was a cell phone. He reached in, grabbed it and held it up.

The cell phone was covered in blood.

Chapter Seven

Inside the Bitterroot Falls police station, Officer Isabella Midthunder drew a sample of Kimi's blood for them to compare against what they'd found on the cell phone at the house. A DNA test would confirm if it was her father's blood.

Kimi was furious with her dad for dropping out of her life only to draw a big target on her back. But she hoped he was okay. No matter what their issues, she'd never want any harm to come to him. She loved him. As complicated and difficult as that love was, it was real.

If nothing else, he'd had the forethought to hire Takoda to keep her safe. Enlisting him meant all of IPS would do whatever they could to protect her. Maybe her father knew her well enough to know that if she ran into trouble, she might hesitate to ask for help.

The note and the retainer he'd sent to Takoda were insurance that her stubbornness wouldn't get her killed.

That was love, as flawed and confusing as it might be. Wasn't it?

Why couldn't it be straightforward and simple with the men in her life?

She glanced over at Takoda. Hunky, sexy, frustrating man. The mixture of hurt and anger simmering in her chest made it hard to breathe.

Takoda was talking to Logan and Lieutenant Midthunder. They were out of earshot, but they had been working on getting representatives from the Cutthroat Creek Mining Company and the Stracke Group to come down to the station as part of procedure, to answer some questions regarding the case.

Both companies, surprisingly, were cooperating, without any red-tape delays, or giving Logan the runaround.

"All done." The officer put a piece of gauze on her arm and then a Band-Aid. She finished labeling the vial of blood.

The younger Midthunder was about Kimi's age. She wore her hair in a sleek bun and had a warm, kind demeanor. Unlike the lieutenant. Not once had she glanced at her father, and the lieutenant had steered clear of his daughter since entering the station. They hadn't even exchanged greetings.

Kimi found the tension interesting. But could she use it to her advantage? "You had such a gentle touch." She pulled down the sleeve of her sweater. "I know a few phlebotomists who could learn a thing or two from you."

The officer smiled.

"Do you mind if I call you Isabella?"

"Sure, but it's just Izzy."

"My father disappearing has been a lot for me. Being followed and attacked hasn't helped. The thing is, we have a strained relationship. You could even call it estranged. There's so much about his current life that he didn't share with me. That he kept hidden." Kimi scooted to the edge of her chair, getting closer to the officer. "Someone on the rez filed a missing person's report for my father. Before I did."

Izzy frowned. "Ouch."

"Exactly." Kimi nodded. Izzy got it. They were making a connection. "Your dad won't tell me who it is and it's driving me nuts. The not knowing who. Or what their relationship is to my dad. I respect the fact that he's entitled to a private life.

But his choices have put me in danger. I may never see him again." That was true, but she hoped that wasn't the case. "I don't even know who's after me or why. I feel like my father stripped me of power by putting me in the dark and in danger without even telling me why. The one thing that would make this horrible time just a little easier, is if I knew who filed the report and what they mean to my father."

Izzy flicked a glance at her own father before lowering her eyes.

"I know I'm asking a lot from you, and we only just met. But I need to take control of my life. My father, Takoda, now your father, who's using his authority to keep information from me that I have a right to know—they're all trying to help, but it feels like I'm being pushed aside." She looked at Izzy. "A name. Their relationship. That's all I need."

Looking up at her, Izzy said nothing.

Kimi grabbed a pen and a sticky note. She wrote down her cell phone number. "Think about it. Will you do that? At least consider it?"

Izzy hesitated. Slid another furtive glance across the room to her father. Lowered her head. She pulled off the latex gloves and tossed them in the waste bin. With a curt nod, she picked up the sticky note and the DNA sample. "I'll consider it," she whispered and walked away.

That was ten times better than a flat-out *no*. Kimi would take it.

PACING INSIDE the observation room of the police department, Kim stared at Lieutenant Joe Midthunder. There was no guarantee that Izzy would try to help her and, even if she did, there was no surety she'd succeed.

A hundred different splintering emotions ricocheted through Kimi. What was the lieutenant hiding? Who was he hiding? Protecting? What gave him the right to decide she didn't have a need to know?

Takoda stepped in front of her, stopping her in her tracks and redirecting her attention. He shook his head. "Let it go." Then he mouthed, *For now.*

There he went, trying to tell her what to do, again. She narrowed her eyes at him.

He flattened his mouth in a grim line. "I'm on your side. Always." The sincerity in his voice almost made her want to forgive him for his rejection earlier.

Almost.

The door opened. Logan came into the room. "Representatives from both companies are here and supposedly eager to cooperate. We'll have to wait and see how true that is."

"It only took them four hours to show up," Kimi said, sounding far snarkier and more sarcastic than she liked.

Logan frowned. "At least we got a same-day response with representatives showing up here at the station, rather than us being forced to go to them, only to get bounced around from one office to the next. This is faster and more efficient."

"I'm sorry." She put a hand on Logan's arm. "You're right."

"Who did they send?" Tak asked.

"We have Phyllis Earle, the senior vice president of legal from the Stracke Group, and Nick Nason, the chief financial officer of CCMC. I'm not thrilled they sent a lawyer, but I expected it. The good news is the Stracke Group only sent one and not a team. All right, Joe, let's go question them."

"If you don't mind," Midthunder said, "I'd prefer to keep my involvement in the investigation discreet. No need to draw unwanted attention to the reservation."

"You mean to the person who filed the report," Kimi said.

The lieutenant didn't even glance in her direction.

"I'll go instead." Tak went up to Logan. "Sit in with you."

Logan considered it for a second. "Will you be in there as a close personal friend of Kimi's or as a professional?"

"Her father hired me to protect her. This is official IPS business. But we all know it's also personal."

The answer seemed to satisfy Logan, and he nodded.

After the two men left, Kimi pivoted on her heel and stared at Joe Midthunder. The man had turned his back to her, like she wasn't even there, and looked through the one-way glass into the interrogation room.

Since she hadn't grown up on the reservation, she didn't know him, but she'd heard of him. He was a hard man but a fair one. Didn't speak unless he had something important to say. And that when you were around him, it was better to listen than to speak.

To hell with that.

First, her father had spent years avoiding her and Jacy like they were mistakes he wanted to forget. Whenever they had talked, it wasn't about anything real. Anything that mattered, at least to her. She had so many questions for her father that she might never get to ask.

Kimi marched up beside Midthunder, ready to get some answers from someone.

"You should listen to your friend," he said, his voice low, his gaze focused on the other room as Logan and Takoda showed Phyllis Earle in and got started. "Let it go."

"The only problem with that is, Takoda doesn't get to tell me what to do and neither do you. Was it some woman my father was seeing who filed the report?"

Silence.

Her blood simmered, her face growing hot. "If it is, you can tell me, Lieutenant Midthunder."

"Call me Joe."

"Whatever you tell me will stay between us," she pleaded.

"I won't share it with Takoda or Logan." Her dad wasn't the only one who could keep a secret. She just wanted the truth. "But I need to know. I need you to tell me for my own sanity."

He turned his head slightly, running his gaze over her face. The line of his mouth was firm, his sharp features unyielding the slightest bit to her honey-coated attempt at persuasion. "You don't know what you need." Hooking his thumbs on his belt, he returned to looking straight ahead. "And I can't give you peace of mind. No one else can do that for you."

Inflexible. Obstinate.

Grinding her teeth, Kimi had had enough of being stonewalled and dismissed where her father was concerned. "I deserve answers!" She caught herself, surprised by her own raised voice, and glanced at the interrogation room to see if they had heard her. No one seemed to as they continued with preliminaries, establishing things for the record.

"You do deserve answers, only not from me," Joe said coolly. "Misplaced anger solves nothing, but can destroy everything." His tone wasn't antagonistic or even condescending, which somehow only irritated her more. Turning, he faced her. Met her gaze and held it. "Be careful. In trying to find your father, don't lose yourself and the things you hold dear along the way." He looked back at the interrogation room.

"You sound like a fortune cookie, Joe."

Not a word in response, but she spotted the corner of his mouth hitch up in a slight grin.

Kimi wanted to scream in frustration, but she controlled herself. Anger had always been easier for her to manage than the alternatives.

Grief. Pain.

Love. The one-sided kind. For her father.

For Takoda.

Tears stung her eyes, but she refused to cry in front of

this man. Straightening, she drew in a deep breath and did her best to focus on the discussion in the interrogation room.

"We did not poach Mr. Wheeler." Phyllis Earle sat poised, wearing a blue pantsuit that was nearly the same color as her eyes, and Kimi thought it was a bold choice for such a conservative-looking woman. She had chestnut hair that was streaked gray and pulled back from her face. "He approached us about a position. I was concerned that he would violate the noncompete clause in his contract with CCMC, which is standard in positions such as his in our industry. He assured us it wouldn't be a problem for him to be released from his contract without any worry that CCMC would seek injunctive relief or monetary or punitive damages."

Nodding, Logan took notes. "Did he have proof of this assurance?"

"No, he didn't."

Logan tilted his head to the side. "Then why take such a risk by hiring him?"

"The matter wasn't clear-cut. There were many factors to consider. Palladium is very rare, making it more expensive than silver, platinum or gold. Mr. Wheeler is a renowned geologist and mining engineer. With his exceptional expertise in pinpointing palladium, the board was willing to gamble on him despite my warning that things could get messy."

"What compensation package did you offer him?" Tak asked.

"Title as chief of the exploration department. A fifty-thousand-dollar signing bonus. Six-figure starting salary. In addition, very lucrative bonuses based on production benchmarks. We agreed to give him a percentage of the revenue on the back end, which is unheard of, but we were willing to pay for his talent. He also asked for something else that was unprecedented. Another stipulation in his contract was that we would consider any current or former employees from CCMC to fill our positions if they applied and didn't have a noncompete clause. I think he wanted us to lure their best folks away. Thomas must have had a big grudge against CCMC."

"Did you ever hear anything from CCMC, receive any legal threats from them regarding his noncompete clause after he was hired?" Logan asked, and Ms. Earle shook her head. "Would it be possible to get a copy of his contract?"

Ms. Earle picked up her phone and typed something. "My assistant will email it shortly."

Logan set down his pen. "When was the last time you saw Thomas?"

"Saturday evening at the gala we hosted in the Bitterroot Mountain Hotel ballroom. We made a big announcement about the first mine we're opening and introduced the entire team to the press. Thomas was so excited. At first. The chief of staff gathered the team backstage, ensuring we were ready to walk on stage when our names were called. Thomas was all smiles. Then he spotted someone near the curtain and his entire demeanor changed. His enthusiasm turned to nerves. After the announcement, it was like he vanished. I couldn't find him anywhere."

Leaning forward, Tak rested his forearms on the table. "Did you get a look at the person he saw backstage?"

She nodded. "It was a man. Tall. On the muscular side. He had facial hair. Not a beard. More of a heavy five-o'clock shadow. I remember him because he was wearing sunglasses at night indoors. It's a pet peeve of mine."

A chill ran through Kimi and she shivered.

Joe looked over at her. "Do you know the person she described?"

"The same man who started following me on Sunday and did this to my face the other day." She gestured to the bruises.

In the interrogation room, Logan's phone chimed and he glanced at the screen. "That was fast. I received a copy of the contract. That's all we have for you for now. If you hear from Thomas, please let us know."

Phyllis Earle stood.

"One more thing," Tak said. "What will you do if Thomas doesn't turn up? Do you have a replacement for him?"

"It would be a significant blow to the Stracke Group. We can start production on the first mine thanks to him. Fortunately, it looks as though it will be very profitable. Current projections forecast that the mine will be operational for at least twenty years. We had big plans for this region, but Thomas was the key to it," Phyllis said. "Now that he's officially missing, the board will have to come up with a contingency plan. It's a shame. Thomas was set to begin surveying a new area next week. If only he had shared whatever he was working on in his notebook before he disappeared." Phyllis shook their hands and left.

The brown leather-bound book her father carried everywhere. They hadn't found it at the house.

"What is it?" Joe asked her. "What are you thinking?"

"That notebook. Instead of using a laptop, like this is the twenty-first century, Dad preferred to write things down." Her mom had given it to him as a present years ago. Personalized with his initials. Whenever he filled it up, he simply replaced the insert with a new packet of paper. "He always had it on him. Maybe that's what those men are looking for. Is this all about palladium?"

"Possibly. It is a billion-dollar industry."

She thought back to the cell phone hidden in the house and the bloody handprint on it. She wondered how long it would take to get back the test results. "Do you think my dad is dead?"

"Not wise to speculate. The blood at the house might not have been your dad's. If he was injured and bleeding, why would he take the time to hide the phone and wipe away any traces of blood on the floor or the dresser? What I know for certain is that you were right about Thomas. He's smart and shrewd. He's a survivor."

But that raised an alarming question. "Well, if the blood isn't his, then whose could it be?"

Joe gave her a steely look. "That's what I've been wondering."

Chapter Eight

Takoda stayed seated in the interrogation room while Logan went to get the next representative. He pulled up the article he'd found about the Stracke Group. It accused them of going into working-class communities rich in natural resources across the globe and establishing a couple of mines. Once they'd been depleted, Stracke closed the mines, leaving the communities in worse conditions than they'd started, but all they cared about was their bottom line.

The deal they'd made with Thomas would've cost them a great deal of revenue. But if they had gotten their hands on his notes, finding the locations for the next mines, then eliminating him would have saved the expense of paying Thomas and potential litigation with CCMC. That would explain why they'd been willing to gamble on Thomas.

Billions were at stake.

What if the man with sunglasses worked for the Stracke Group? What if something went wrong and Thomas got away with his notebook?

The door to the interrogation room opened. Logan ushered in Nick Nason, the CFO of Cutthroat Creek Mining Company. They both sat.

"This is Takoda Yazzie, from Ironside Protection Services. He'll be sitting in on the interview." Logan went through preliminary questions, getting Nason to state his full name and title for the record since the interview was being recorded. "Not to offend you, Mr. Nason, but we were expecting someone from your legal department to come in. Maybe even the chief of staff."

"My thoughts exactly," Nason said. "But the CEO, Jeff Randolph, asked me to come. Lately, with all the bad press regarding the layoffs, it's been me and legal as the face of the company."

"How long did Thomas Wheeler work for CCMC?" Logan asked.

"A long time." Leaning back in his chair, Nason crossed his legs and smoothed down the front of his expensive-looking suit. "Almost thirty-five years. Longer even than I have been with the company."

Logan nodded. "Was he a good employee?"

"One of the best. He made a valuable contribution for many years before leaving."

"When was the last time you saw him?" Logan asked.

"The day he quit," Nason said. "He turned in his letter of resignation at the holiday office party, which was held on the twentieth. Made a big spectacle of it."

Based on what they'd heard of his reputation so far, her father sounded like the type who would've given at least two weeks' notice. Unless he couldn't for some reason. Had he resigned in the middle of a public office party instead of behind closed doors because it was safer?

Tak tried to connect the dots from the resignation to Thomas days later meeting Kimi to give her those presents. According to Kimi, her father even went so far as to put the necklace on her, as though he feared she might not bother to take it out of the box.

All of those things were connected: the resignation, the new job, the presents. They had to be. But how?

"Thomas spent over thirty years working for CCMC," Takoda said. "Any idea why he would he leave, especially so abruptly? Was it work conditions? Salary?"

Nason shoved a hand through his hair. It was thick and dark, less flecked with gray than Phyllis Earle's. He looked to be younger than the lawyer, maybe in his late forties. "Only Thomas could tell you for certain, but he did ask for several pay raises in the past five years. Every time, we increased his salary by two percent, and he always received a twenty-five-thousand-dollar bonus with each new target area he discovered for us."

They weren't paying Thomas what he was worth. A two percent raise didn't even keep pace with inflation. Takoda studied the CFO's face, his body language. "Twenty-five grand for a site that would bring in millions."

Nason gave a pleasant smile, though he couldn't quite manage to make his eyes look remotely pleasant. "I'm sorry. I didn't hear a question."

Takoda folded his hands in his lap. "Why wasn't Thomas paid more? Why wasn't he given perks and better bonuses?"

Nason rested his elbows on the arms of his chair and made a confident steeple of his fingertips. "In mining, it's a balancing act between risk and reward. The company takes all the risks and deals with the financial setbacks while keeping things operational. It was Thomas's job to lead exploration and find spots for new mines. Palladium is typically deeper and harder to locate and access than, say, gold or silver. Sometimes we won't get a highly conductive electromagnetic response over target areas. That's where Thomas came in. His sixth sense was uncanny. Reliable. If he told us where to dig, we usually hit paydirt every single time. But with the last two sites he selected, we were never able to confirm the presence of palladium or any other precious metal that we could've used. Consequently, we didn't recoup the expense of the exploration. Thomas cost us millions in addition to the waste of time and other resources."

"There's been talk in the town and articles in the *Bitterroot Beacon* about the recent layoffs," Logan said. "Is the loss in revenue from the failed sites Thomas picked the reason?"

"Yes, in part. We laid off two hundred workers because of him. We've also automated certain divisions with advancements in technology, and had to let another hundred and fifty workers go for that reason. Machines are cheaper in the long run. We had to reduce production costs. According to the chief of operations, Thomas had lost his magic touch. He became a dud. We allowed him to leave to mitigate our future losses."

Logan flipped through his notepad. "After the Stracke Group hired Thomas, he found a lucrative target area for them. The mine is projected to be operational for twenty years. I'm sure CCMC isn't happy about being wrong about him. Was anyone so bitter about that they might seek revenge?"

"Thomas found one mine for them." Nason shrugged, like that meant nothing. "It's only a matter of time before the Stracke Group realizes who they really hired. A dud."

"Maybe you'd like us to believe he lost his magic touch because it fits the narrative for CCMC." Logan closed his notebook. "Your company lost millions in revenue and laid off hundreds of people, only to watch your competitor celebrate a lucrative new mine thanks to Thomas Wheeler. Maybe someone in the company was so upset over seeing him produce for the Stracke Group instead of CCMC, they took measures to ensure the one mine Thomas found for them would also be the last."

Another pleasant smile that didn't reach Nason's eyes. "I

hear a lot of speculation, but no proof. More importantly, no question."

Takoda refrained from shaking his head as he listened to Nason. The guy might be the chief financial officer, but he acted like a lawyer, only answering questions asked, deftly steering clear of being baited. "What's your background? What did you do before working for CCMC?"

"I was a lawyer with the securities and exchange commission. I was looking for a change and wanted to move back home to Montana. A friend of a friend recommended me for a position at Cutthroat Creek Mining and I've been with them ever since."

Explained a lot. "You didn't mention you were a lawyer," Takoda said.

"You didn't ask."

Both TSG and CCMC were being careful, which was to be expected.

"After Thomas hit paydirt for the Stracke Group," Logan said, "why didn't you sue him for breach of contract since he had a noncompete clause?"

Nason sighed. "I was hoping I wouldn't have to bring this up, but Thomas was not only a dud, quite frankly, he was dangerous to be around."

Takoda straightened. "What do you mean?"

"He was in debt to a loan shark," Nason said. "I assumed Thomas had a gambling problem based on rumors and his nickname—Wheeler Dealer. He became a liability to the company. There was a clause in his contract that stipulated if he was terminated for any reason, he would get a big payday. That was drafted before I came on board. We were happy to accept his resignation instead of shelling out more money to a lost cause."

Logan and Takoda exchanged a look. Neither of them had

heard any whispers of Thomas Wheeler being in debt. Besides, only a fool went to a loan shark for money, and Kimi's father was no fool.

"That's a significant claim," Logan said. "Any proof to substantiate it?"

"Big Billy Burdock. Have you heard of him?" Nason asked, and both Tak and Logan nodded. "Burdock confronted Thomas on company grounds and assaulted another employee who tried to intervene."

Logan picked up his pen. "The name of this other employee?"

"After his nose was broken, the individual has made it clear that he doesn't want to have anything to do with Thomas or his troubles, but his name is Peter O'Donnell. We do have a recording of the altercation from a security camera." Nason took out his phone and quickly hit Play, as though he'd had the video teed up and ready to go. He set the phone on the table.

On the screen, Thomas Wheeler left a mine and was striding through the parking lot when Burdock hopped out of a pickup truck, ambushing him. Burdock was stocky and bald and smaller than someone might expect with the moniker Big Billy.

There was no audio on the playback, but it was clear they were having a heated conversation. If only Takoda could hear what it was about. The time and date stamp in the upper right corner showed December 15, 4:35 p.m.

In the video, Big Billy grabbed Thomas by his shirt and yelled at him. Pointed a thick, meaty finger at his face.

The loan shark had a nasty reputation, but desperate people still turned to him for help. Only to regret it later. There were rumors that if his clients didn't pay him what they owed, they would end up with broken bones. Sometimes family members were threatened. In worst-case scenarios, those clients who failed to pay disappeared.

No body, no murder charge. Convicting someone of murder without the purported victim's body in evidence was theoretically possible. But it was extremely hard to prove, forcing the prosecution to rely on circumstantial evidence. Also, where Burdock was concerned, no one was ever willing to testify against him.

For two minutes, the argument continued as Thomas raised a shaky palm and appeared to try and reason with Burdock.

Takoda noticed that in Wheeler's other hand, he was clutching a brown leather-bound book close to his side. The one with his notes about the palladium mines.

Then another man appeared on the screen. A guy wearing a hard hat ran over and made the mistake of trying to pull Burdock off Kimi's father. His back was to the surveillance camera, making it hard to identify him. Burdock punched the man in the face. The hard hat flew off from the impact of the blow, and the man cradled his face, which still wasn't visible, in his hands—maybe his nose was broken. Burdock shoved Thomas to ground, got back in his truck, and sped out of the lot.

Once the video finished, Nason said, "I'd be happy to forward this to you."

No doubt the finance lawyer would do so quickly.

Logan nodded. "Yes, we'll need it." He passed his number to Nason, and within seconds Logan's phone chimed with the receipt.

Tak crossed his arms, hating the fact they were left with more questions than answers. "Mr. Nason, why didn't CCMC file charges against Burdock after the assault for battery, or the very least, trespassing?"

"Burdock is not a man to be trifled with," Nason said.

"He was only on CCMC property because of Thomas. We don't want any problems around our mines or with any of our employees. Burdock is a man known for causing trouble. If Thomas went to work for a different company, then the loan shark would stay off CCMC property and away from our employees. No need to stir up more problems, antagonizing a ruthless thug by filing charges. The violent incident was only one more reason we were relieved to wash our hands of Thomas."

After Nick Nason stood and left, Tak and Logan rejoined the others in the observation room.

Joe turned to Kimi. "Did you know about your father's gambling debts?"

"No," she said, shaking her head, "but then there is a lot about him that I don't know. Whoever filed the missing person's report might know more. You should ask them."

"I will."

Kimi stared at Joe, her eyes narrowed, her hands clenched.

"Try to remember," Joe said, softening his expression and his tone, "I'm not the man you're furious with."

Takoda felt like he had missed something. The tension between Kimi and Joe was different, but not necessarily better.

She had a right to be upset, at her father, at him after the way he handled everything in the kitchen. *Tactless Tak strikes again.* But she didn't have a right to take it out on Joe. He was only doing his job, and his responsibility was to protect the people on the Bigfork Reservation.

"Now we have some leads to go on," Logan said. "I'll start with questioning Peter O'Donnell. See if he caught any part of the conversation between Thomas and Burdock. We know the man who has been following you was at the Bitterroot Mountain Hotel on Saturday evening. He should be on the security footage. We may be able to get a good image of him and figure out who he is. As for Burdock, he's a known loan shark, with a couple of convictions for misdemeanors. We haven't been able to charge him with any felonies. Definitely the type of man who would break kneecaps if someone owed him money. Finding him might be tricky, but I'll make it my top priority."

"Can we see the video Nason showed you?" Kimi asked.

Logan brought it up for her and Joe to watch.

Focused on the screen, Kimi tensed. When it came to the part where Burdock got violent, she cringed.

Logan stopped the playback of the recording. "I'm sorry you had to see that."

So was Tak. She might have a difficult relationship with her father, even be angry with him for putting her in this deadly situation, but Takoda was certain that if anything bad happened to Thomas, it would hurt her.

DISBELIEF CLOUDED EVERYTHING. Kimi wasn't certain what was true anymore. She reeled from the video. Was her father a gambling addict? Indebted to a vicious loan shark?

She would've sworn it wasn't possible. Until she'd watched Burdock threaten her father.

"In the video, Dad is holding the notebook that Ms. Earle mentioned," she said. "I didn't see it at the house. The men who tossed my place and Dad's might've been looking for it. He keeps all his research notes in there. I'm sure whatever location he was going to survey next would be in his notebook."

Takoda nodded. "That would make it worth a lot of money."

He was right. So much money that it might be worth killing to get it.

Someone cleared their throat, and everyone looked at the doorway. Chief Edgar Macon stood in the hall. The man was burly with a barrel chest. His graying hair was cropped tight and low. He strode into the room with the full force of his authority sucking up the air around them.

"Logan, we need to have a word about the Wheeler case. In private."

"Should Joe be a part of the conversation?" Logan asked.

"No." The chief looked around the room. "Excuse us."

Joe led the way out. Kimi and Tak followed him down the hall. The door to the observation room closed.

"What do you think that's all about?" Kimi asked.

"No way of knowing," Joe said. "No need to speculate. You two appear to be very chummy with Detective Powell. I'm sure he'll fill you in."

Raised voices came from the observation room. The heated conversation was short. Chief Macon left, not making eye contact with them as he stormed past.

A few seconds later, Logan joined them at the end of the hall, looking flustered and shell-shocked. "I'm off the case."

Surprise slid through Kimi like cold water rushing in her veins. "What? Why?"

"I wasn't given a reason." Logan shook his head, his eyes still dazed, his cheeks red. "The chief made it clear he didn't have to give me one."

"Who is taking over the case?" Tak asked.

Logan rubbed his forehead. "No one."

"But my father is missing," Kimi said. This was all so surreal. "Joe has a missing person's report, and I filed one with the BFPD. You can't just drop it. This is an official case."

"Not anymore." Logan's jaw clenched as he glanced at them. "I was *ordered* to stand down. If the blood on the phone turns out to be your father's, then the chief might possibly reconsider. He emphasized *possibly*. Until then, no other BFPD resources are to be used on the Thomas Wheeler case."

Kimi heaved a sigh and then pivoted toward Joe. "What about you? You'll continue to investigate, won't you?"

"My authority is limited to Bigfork and, as I've already told you, I don't want to draw unwanted attention."

"This is unbelievable." She threw her hands up in the air. "So, you all are just giving up?"

"I'm not." The sincerity in Takoda's voice drew her full attention. "We'll figure this out together, with the IPS team. Protecting you means finding out what happened to your father."

"But we both recognize it's useful to have someone with a badge to help," she said. "You've pointed out to me numerous times where IPS had to rely on law enforcement to get a warrant."

Takoda said nothing in response.

What argument could he make? The power of a warrant was a mighty thing, and as capable as IPS was, they didn't have the authority to get one.

"You still have a badge working on your behalf," Joe said coolly.

"What are you talking about?" Kimi asked, not filtering the irritation from her voice.

"*He*," Joe said, pointing a finger at Logan, "was kicked off the Thomas Wheeler case. Not the Kimi Redbird Wheeler case. The guy with the sunglasses may have been after your dad, but he also followed you. Attacked you. If Takoda can't convince the hotel to share the footage from the night of the Stracke Group gala, Powell can still get a warrant without mentioning Thomas. And Burdock trespassed on private property and assaulted someone in addition to your dad. That gives Powell a reason to look into Burdock, too. Maybe the loan shark's flunkies are after you. Who knows. But while the good detective is questioning Burdock, if Thomas's name happens to come up in a discussion, I'd call that a happy coincidence."

As far as Kimi was concerned, there was nothing happy about any of this. But she supposed she couldn't find a hole in his logic.

"No matter where this leads," Tak said to her, "I'm in this with you. Not because of the retainer from your dad. And not because Jacy would haunt me if I didn't help." He stopped, not actually telling her why.

Leaving her to wonder. But she believed him.

The one thing she was sure of was that he wasn't going to abandon her this time, and he wasn't going to give up.

"A word of caution," Joe said, lowering his voice to a whisper. "Whatever the reason behind Ed Macon ordering Logan to drop the case, it's a problem. I suggest you find out how big of one if you're going to pursue this."

Kimi followed Tak's gaze across the bullpen to the chief's office. Ed Macon was sitting behind his desk, on the phone, staring at them.

Was the chief of the Bitterroot Falls PD dirty?

Or was the problem much worse?

Chapter Nine

This was an all-hands-on-deck kind of scenario. Gathering the rest of the Ironside Protection Services team was essential and Takoda didn't waste any time doing it.

Not only had Eli, Bo, Chance and Autumn shown up, but the entire crew came to the Wolverine Lodge. Logan and Summer, a lawyer who made her mark in the area with a prominent case. Chance's significant other Winter also joined them, along with her colleague Declan Hart. Both Winter and Declan were DOJ Division of Criminal Investigation special agents. Kimi finally got to meet Bo's girlfriend, Nora Santana, a previous IPS client.

Even Jackson Powell, Logan's brother came. The US marshal lived in Missoula. They usually only saw him for big events or for brunch on occasion when he was free.

All their lives intersected and intermingled, and they had become more than coworkers or friends. They were family. In a time of need, they stuck together and had each other's backs.

The Wolverine Lodge was conveniently located for everyone, and the food was great. Also, their table received a couple of plates of appetizers on the house. Summer and Logan were sort of local celebrities after they'd stopped a local company from selling a product that was poisoning people. IPS had helped Summer to comb through the mountain of discovery material. In the end, she'd received a huge settlement to compensate those who had gotten sick.

They had pushed several smaller tables together in the bar section of the restaurant. Service was faster for their large group when they placed their orders through the bartender and picked things up as they were ready, bringing everything back to the table themselves.

Watching Kimi light up at seeing the crew tugged at Takoda's heart. She needed them all more than ever: their kindness, their support, and their love.

He hadn't realized how much she had missed out on after he had distanced himself, and thereby also the group, from her. New relationships, engagement parties and meeting relatives from out of town, the holidays, group dinners and Sunday brunches. Kimi hadn't participated in any of it because of him.

Takoda felt like the biggest jerk.

Going forward, he vowed to himself that no matter what happened between him and Kimi, never again would he put her in a position where she felt that she had to alienate herself from all these people who cared about her.

Once Kimi had gotten through hugging everyone and catching up on their lives, they dug into their food and delved into the nuances of the situation with Thomas Wheeler.

"Have you reached out to your mom yet?" Summer asked.

Kimi nodded. "I called. Left several messages and sent her a text." She shrugged. "Now, I have to wait. Unlike my father, my mom is good at calling back. If not within the same day, then by the next at the latest. Unless she's hiking or camping somewhere with lousy cell service."

Worry furrowed Kimi's brow. Takoda wanted to rewind the clock a few minutes to when she was smiling and happy to be surrounded by trustworthy people determined to help her. Not focused entirely on the dire details of their predicament.

Maybe if they all put their brains together, they could bounce around theories and get one step closer to figuring out what on earth was going on.

"Kimi, if your dad was hiding, any idea where he would go?" Jackson sat across from her. He'd been quiet since he arrived, taking everything in. Studying every answer and response like he was just as eager to uncover the truth.

A professional habit none of them could break.

Kimi shrugged. "He's lived in Bitterroot Falls all his life. I know when my mom was pregnant with Jacy, they talked about moving to the Bigfork Reservation, where she grew up, but they decided against it for some reason. But I know he's not there staying with anyone."

"How can you be sure?" Jackson asked.

"Lieutenant Midthunder from the reservation PD is looking for him, too. Someone there filed a missing person's report, but he won't tell me who." Kimi looked down at her food, her shoulders tensing.

Tak ached to comfort her, but he was always more cognizant, more careful, around the group.

"That must be hard." Seated on the other side of Kimi, Nora put a hand on her arm. "While you wait for your mom to send the necklace," Nora said, changing the subject, "at least you have the book your dad gave you. It might be the key to a lead, right?"

"Where my father is concerned, anything is possible." Kimi slid a look at Takoda.

He pulled on a hopeful smile. "I think the probability it's important is high. I don't buy it was a coincidence he gave you the book and necklace, then disappeared a few weeks later without it being connected."

"I still can't believe the chief pulled you from the case," Declan said to Logan. "With zero explanation."

Logan grimaced and tipped his beer up to his lips. Summer put a hand on his back and rubbed. "The sooner we can get the DNA samples analyzed the better," Logan said. "If the blood turns out to be Thomas's, I'll have a fighting chance of getting it reopened."

"The DCI lab will run it faster," Winter said. "One of us can take it over and have it processed."

"I'll do it," Declan offered. "Tonight."

"Are you sure?" Winter asked. "I don't mind going."

The DCI lab was an hour-and-a-half-drive away in Missoula.

"Go home with Chance," Declan said. "This single guy will take the hit."

Autumn glanced at Declan. The look had been so quick, so subtle, so full of sympathy, that if anyone hadn't been paying close attention, they would've missed it. Tak didn't think there was anything going on between the two since Autumn had a boyfriend. The professor was notably absent tonight, as usual. But part of Tak believed Autumn and Declan would've made a better match.

"How about if you let this single guy do it?" Jackson offered. "I was going to hang around for a few days since I have time, but I can run it to the lab. Sleep at home there. Come back tomorrow and pitch in any way I can to help find Kimi's dad."

"Appreciate it," Declan said. "But if you're coming back tomorrow, you should probably count on staying with Logan and Summer. A nasty storm is coming in. Supposed to hit by late afternoon."

"Hey, Chance, how well do you know Ed Macon?" Takoda asked. Chance was in charge of the IPS Big Sky office, had been in Bitterroot Falls the longest, and had worked on a couple of cases with Macon. It was because of him that IPS had cemented such a strong professional relationship with the BFPD. "I'm trying to wrap my head around why he'd pull Logan from the case the way he did."

Chance finished chewing and wiped his hands on a napkin. "He has a solid history of being trustworthy and on the up and up. I've never heard any whispers of corruption. *But* I do think anyone could be compromised under the right circumstances."

Dissenting opinions rose around the table for a few chaotic minutes.

"Not you," Winter said. She kissed Chance's cheek. "You could never be corrupted. Not for money or power. You're too good. I daresay everyone at this table is."

"What about for love?" asked Autumn, a forensic psychologist who'd once worked as a profiler for the FBI. "I think most of you would do anything to protect the person you loved. Even if it meant compromising yourself. Am I wrong?"

A couple of heads lowered, along with some forks, but no one disagreed.

The hairs along the back of Takoda's neck rose. The bustle slowed, along with everything inside him. The din muted and everyone at the table around him faded, even Kimi. Setting his glass of water down, he surveyed the room. He wasn't sure what he was looking for, and maybe it was nothing.

Look harder and you'll see, Jacy said, his voice razor-sharp.

Two things Tak never ignored: his instincts and the voice of his dead best friend. Rubbing the back of his neck, he scanned the room again, slowly this time.

Then he spotted it. *Right there.*

At the end of the bar, the section in a corner with dim lighting. Tak's gaze clashed with a cold, dark stare in the mirror behind the bar. A man dressed in a black business shirt and slacks, sitting on a stool. Not a big guy, like the one Kimi had described who'd followed her. This man was tall, lean and hard, the outline of sinewy muscles obvious in the shirt that fit him like a glove. His hair was cropped so low, a tattoo on the back of his head was visible.

The guy cut his gaze from the mirror and picked up his drink. More tats across his knuckles.

Takoda wanted to dismiss the sensation of alarm firing up his nerve endings as paranoia. Perhaps an overreaction. But the feeling wouldn't leave him. In fact, it only intensified the more he thought about it. The mysterious stranger had a distinct hardness about the eyes, one that marked someone devoid of goodness, or empathy, or some might even call it a soul. Sure, he'd crossed paths with bad people and that was part of the reason he couldn't shake this.

Not when he had a nagging sense of familiarity. Tak had never seen him before, but he had encountered his particular type.

Deadly. Someone who would not hesitate to take a life if it got them closer to achieving their objective.

Tak didn't want to inadvertently provoke anything, so he shifted his gaze from the man. Even though he remained hyperaware of his presence, he hoped like hell that guy was not some new giant X factor in their current problem set.

The situation they were dealing with was already big and complicated and didn't need to get any messier. Thomas had hired Takoda to protect Kimi, but the exact nature of the danger, how deep it ran, the number of people involved, and the source of the threat still needed to be cleared up.

Takoda forced himself to tune back into the conversation at the table.

Bo wrapped an arm around Nora's shoulder, and she looked at him like he was the greatest person on the planet. "Autumn made a good point. We'd bend the rules to keep the people we love safe."

Tak turned his attention to Kimi and an ache sliced through him.

She's just my best friend's little sister, he tried to remind himself. Nothing more.

After the kiss this morning, one that had been mutual, making it impossible for him to dismiss his part in it, he was finding it harder to ignore his feelings for her.

Takoda needed to help her, protect her, and not cross the line again.

He flicked a glance at the bar. The tattooed stranger appeared entirely focused on his drink. But Tak knew better.

"Big difference between bending rules and breaking the law," Eli said. "The chief of police made a detective drop a case for no good reason. The question we should be asking is, if Macon is such a good cop, how could he be compromised?"

Chance took another bite of his food, looking around the table. "Well," he said, his tone suggesting the possibility was real, "his wife works for the Cutthroat Creek Mining Company. In human resources."

"Great." Kimi sighed. "How long has she been there?"

Chance frowned. "Maybe thirty years."

"We've got to dig into it," Eli said. "CCMC might have gotten to the chief of police, coerced him or bribed him to drop the case. If they did, we need to know."

Bo nodded. "I agree, but proving it will be hard, and it'll take time. The kind of time Kimi might not have. We should simply operate on the assumption that he's dirty, for now, and once we know she's safe, then we can revisit it. Since the DNA will be processed at the DCI lab, for the sake of expediency, whether or not Macon is on CCMC's payroll doesn't change the landscape other than restricting Logan. We get to the point where someone is caught and can be arrested, I say we call DCI. Meaning you two." Bo gestured to Declan and Winter, and both special agents grinned.

"On the bright side," Logan said, "we were able to get hotel security footage. It didn't shed much light on what happened to Kimi's father, but we were able to pull an image of the man who's been following her. No warrant necessary. Now, we just have to figure out who he is."

"I may know someone who'd be willing to help." Chance set his fork down. "On my last IPS business trip, someone from the Denver office introduced me to a hacker. Guy named Orson. No last name given. Wicked talented. He has a facial recognition program that puts what law enforcement can do to shame, and in less time. But it'll cost us."

Another twinge crawled across the back of Takoda's neck. He looked up and caught the man at the bar staring again. This time the guy held his gaze, steady without blinking, as he finished his drink. Pulled a wad of money from his pocket. Dropped a couple of bills on the bar.

Declan leaned close to Takoda. "What is it?"

Always discreet and alert, Declan had similar instincts, easily picking up on trouble.

"See the guy at the end of the bar. The one with the tats," Takoda whispered, and Declan nodded. "He's been watching us for some reason, and I'm telling you it's not a good one. He's going to try to leave, but we're going to ask him a few questions instead."

Tak and Declan both rose from the table just as the tattooed stranger leisurely lifted himself from the stool and threw on a slim-fit wool coat.

"Where are you going?" Kimi asked.

"Be back in a minute. Need a drink?" Takoda asked, already moving when she shook her head. Takoda went around one side of the table to cut off the guy while Declan approached from the other side to outflank him.

The stranger slipped a hand in his pocket and turned, facing them. He stood still and shook his head once. A sharp and clear motion of warning.

Takoda's gaze dropped when the man flashed the inside of his coat, the hand in the pocket raised slightly, subtly. He noticed the rigid, telltale outline of a gun pressing against the inner lining of the stranger's coat pocket. Not simply a gun. From the length of it, the shape, and the fact only the man's fingers barely fit in the pocket, it was one with an attached sound suppressor.

Plenty of folks in Montana carried a gun.

A *silencer* changed the game. It meant this guy was a professional. A mercenary. A hired gun. Killing a person *was* the mission.

Tak halted several tables away from the man.

Declan spotted it, too, and stopped moving.

The gun wasn't pointed at Tak or Declan. It was aimed in the direction of their table. At Kimi. Where the others sat, five of them with their backs to what was transpiring—all of them vulnerable to being shot.

Impotent fury flooded Tak, hot and fierce. He stood rooted to the spot, not daring to even twitch a finger when there was a gun trained on the people he loved.

The deadly stranger leveled his gaze at him and smiled, the expression full of menace and meaning.

That guy had the upper hand, quite literally with his finger on the trigger, while Takoda and Declan were at a severe disadvantage, even though they had the numbers and firepower on their side.

This was no bluff. No test. It was a checkmate. If they pressed this and tried to confront him, Kimi could take a bullet. Any of their friends or number of innocent bystanders in the restaurant could be killed.

Then chaos would ensue and all bets would be off.

Not going to happen. Not if Tak had the power to prevent it.

With his blood boiling, he watched the man ease backward out of the bar. Staring at them, the stranger strode through the waiting area that was empty and past the hostess station. As soon as the stranger shoved through the front door of the restaurant and headed down the stairs, where he wouldn't have a shot at the bar, both Tak and Declan took off after him. They each drew their weapons along the way.

The cold, hard steel of his Mk 23 in Tak's palm fortified his determination to get that guy. He heard the heavy footfalls of some of the others from their group pounding close on his heels. The unmistakable sound of someone chambering a round into their gun echoed behind him. They burst through the door of the restaurant and raced down the front steps.

Chance, Eli, Winter and Jackson had sprung into action, joining them. Bo's and Logan's instinct would've been to stay at the table, to safeguard their significant others and, of course, Kimi.

Using a hand signal, Takoda directed everyone to split up. Immediately, they fanned out in the parking lot, covering every direction. They peeked in vehicles. Checked every dark corner. Searched behind the restaurant.

No cars sped out of the lot. No sound of anyone running in retreat.

And there was no sign of the tattooed stranger who'd had the audacity to threaten their entire team. To point a gun at Kimi. The man had done so without an inkling of fear. Only a deadness in his eyes and a smile on his face.

In his gut, Takoda knew that this tattooed guy might be the greatest threat.

The one and only consolation was that in the stranger's boldness, he'd exposed himself to the security cameras in the restaurant. Now, they could get a picture of his face to pass to the hacker, Orson. Hopefully, he was as talented as Chance claimed because Takoda doubted the stranger would pop up in normal databases.

This mess Thomas Wheeler had set into motion and dragged them all into kept growing, changing and shifting. Getting deadlier every step of the way.

Kimi had already been followed, attacked, her home tossed and just been in the crosshairs of a new player on the board. All in two days.

Thomas, what have you done?

Whatever happened next, Takoda needed to be ready for it.

Chapter Ten

Tossing in bed, Kimi couldn't sleep. Not for lack of trying.

At first, she was cold in just the T-shirt, so she'd put on the sweatpants that she'd deliberately neglected to wear this morning. Just to mess with Takoda. Or tempt him.

Probably both.

But now she was too warm and still cold at the same time.

She was exhausted, mentally and physically. Being mugged and followed and worried if her father was dead or alive was draining.

Everything could be boiled down to one central problem. She was angry and scared.

Mostly scared. One hundred percent terrified the trouble chasing her was going to catch her and try to kill her.

Not without a fight.

Some people froze when they were frightened. Not her. She usually swung first and asked questions later. As she got older, the jabs became more verbal in nature. Her mom used to say that she should've named her something that meant little warrior instead of little butterfly.

Her phone rang. She glanced at the screen. *About time.* "Hi, Mom," she answered. "Thanks for finally calling me back."

"Kimi, sweetie, you left three messages. Is everything all right?"

Each voicemail had been vague but conveyed a sense of urgency. Every time she tried to think of what to say, it sounded complicated in her head. And scary. The last thing she wanted to do was worry her mother when she had no answers, no idea what was going on, or what had happened to her father.

Too many people were already touched by this. Tonight, the entire IPS team and their significant others had gotten sucked in, too. If she could keep her mother out of it and safe, then she would.

"You know the necklace Dad gave me that I sent to you?"

"Yeah, sweetie. What about it?"

"I need to get it back."

"Oh, I knew you'd come around and want it someday. I know your father is a difficult man to understand, but he loves you."

"Could've fooled me."

Her mom tsked. "Stop that. With the family you're born into, you have to take the love people are able to give and make peace with it."

Kimi lay back and stared at the ceiling, thinking of Takoda. He was loyal. Passionate. Not only in the romantic sense, but in the depth of his convictions.

She suspected a lot of women were attracted to that dangerous air he possessed. But for any of them catching him and holding on to him was the challenge.

"You know," her mom said, "there was a time when you and your dad were really close. You were about nine or ten, and Jacy was a teenager only interested in sports and girls. But you were daddy's little girl. The two of you would collect rocks and test soils and make up codes. Work on those jigsaw puzzles for hours. Do you remember?"

Her heart squeezed. They used to leave each other coded messages and put together 5,000-piece puzzles while her mother baked, painted and played music. Those were the best times. "Yeah. I do. As long as I was interested in something he loved, it was great. The minute I asked him to do something I wanted to do, then he suddenly didn't have the time for me."

Slowly, resentments had fueled anger, and that anger had built a wall between them. One where they'd stopped talking to each other about the things that mattered. Stopped making time to spend together. Letting distance creep in like a terminal disease.

Where was her fight then? Where was her dad's fight?

She was just a kid. Wasn't it on him?

"I hope the fact that since you want the necklace back, it means you're ready to forgive your father for all his mistakes and start over."

Nope, sorry to disappoint you, Mom. "Tomorrow, can you send it to me overnight mail?"

"Oh, sweetie, I wish I could, but the necklace is at home."

"The house here in Montana?"

"No, home as in Spokane."

Of course. Davey's place was now her mother's home. "Where are you?"

"Davey and I are still in Hawaii. Didn't I tell you?"

Kimi stifled a groan. "No, Mom. You didn't."

"Well, we are." Her mother's voice was full of glee. "For two more weeks. The weather is perfect. We went scuba diving today. Tomorrow, we're going surfing."

"That sounds like fun." It really did. At least, she was far away from any danger. "Mom, it's important I get the necklace, for reasons I don't want to explain right now, but I need it ASAP."

"Then I guess you're going to have to go get it. You know the address. A spare key is under the big flowerpot with the winter pansies. The code to the alarm is 3543. And the necklace is in my jewelry case in the top-right dresser drawer."

Davey's place was a retreat outside the city, situated atop a mountain on ten serene acres, with a gorgeous view of Spokane Valley, Liberty Lake and Newman Lake.

"Okay." It was Kimi's fault for not keeping the necklace in the first place. She wasn't a kid anymore and she couldn't keep blaming her dad for the status of things between them. Maybe it was time to forgive old grievances. Figure out a way forward with her father. If he was still alive. And if she survived whatever trouble he had gotten her roped into. "I miss you."

"I miss you, too. You should've come out and spent Christmas with us."

"Intrude on the love bubble during the holidays?" She'd visited them once, not realizing what she was walking into with her mom and Davey. They couldn't keep their hands off each other. The idea of being a third wheel again made Kimi cringe. "No, thanks."

"You're my little warrior, not an intrusion. Not ever. I've got to go, sweetie. Davey made reservations for a romantic dinner on the beach, and he doesn't want us to be late."

"What time is it there?"

"Seven."

Three hours behind. "I won't keep you. Enjoy dinner."

"I will. Love you, sweetie, and I hope you'll think about reaching out to your father. It is a two-way street. You and Thomas used to share so much. In a lot of ways, you're both alike. I'm sure you can find common ground."

That common ground was a part of a different life. Her dad was much closer to someone else. "Hey, Mom, do you know if Dad was seeing anyone on the Bigfork reservation?"

"I don't know. We haven't spoken since Jacy's funeral.

But it's possible. He knows a lot of people out there. Geology takes him everywhere. I've got to go."

"Bye. Love you."

She hung up and rolled over. Her arm hit something hard. The hardbound copy of *The Wizard of Oz* her dad had given her. After all the commotion at the restaurant, with some armed man watching the group, they had forgotten about the book.

Everyone's focus had shifted to a potential new threat. To make matters worse, the security cameras outside the Wolverine Lodge had been disabled, which most of the group believed substantiated Takoda's theory that the mysterious man with tattoos was a professional. And not the good kind. They had gotten a partial image of the man's face from the surveillance system inside the bar, but the guy had acted aware of the cameras and never turned directly toward them.

Takoda was probably awake in his room waiting to hear back from Orson, the hacker Chance had reached out to in the hope of identifying Mr. Sunglasses and Mr. Tattoos.

Besides, she had doubts about whether the book would even lead to a clue. It was entirely possible her dad had given her a first-edition collection of folktales to remind her of better times between them. When they had been close, like her mom had said.

Sitting up, she grabbed the copy of *The Wizard of Oz* and flipped through the pages slowly. Maybe her father had hidden a message inside. She searched the pages for any markings, any dog-eared sections. Perhaps a handwritten phrase. A word. A number. Any clues scribbled on the inner margins.

Zilch.

She sucked in an irritated breath.

KISS, Kimi. Jacy's voice was loud in her head. *Keep it simple, silly.*

A principle in the military and one her brother had used all the time.

Keep it simple. She ran her hand over the cover of the book. Single-layered foiling. The pages had silver-edged gilding. Then she noticed the way the light from the bedside table lamp hit it. How the edges of the pages shimmered.

Like…palladium instead of silver?

She opened the front flap and examined it. The pastedown had a geometric pattern. There was something about the 3-D shape, but she couldn't pinpoint what was bothering her.

On the title page, there was no note. Struck her as odd. During her formative years, her dad had given her plenty of books, mostly about geology and cryptography, but he'd always inscribed them with her name, the date, the occasion, and signed them.

Kimi turned back to the pastedown and smoothed her palm over the geometric-patterned paper. The notion of damaging a book, a first edition no less, went against the way she'd been raised, but desperate times… She reached into one of her bags and pulled out a metal nail file.

Going slowly, she eased the stainless-steel tip under the corner edge of the leaf attached to the inside of the cover. She shimmied it along the edge until the entire endpaper that had been glued to the board was loosened. Nothing. No hidden message for her.

"This is pointless," she muttered to herself, ready to hurl the book across the room.

Don't stop, Jacy said. *Keep digging.*

Something inside Kimi calmed. "Okay, Jacy."

She flipped the book and opened the back flap. Stared at the same geometric pattern. She ran her palm over it. As smooth and level as the front pastedown. She repeated the process of loosening the endpaper from the board. She peeled back the pastedown. Once again, nothing.

Her dad had given her the book for a reason. It wasn't to remind his thirty-year-old daughter of her childhood. Of that, she was certain.

Kimi held the book and looked at the spine. Opening the front and back covers, she studied the joint, the small groove that ran vertically down the book itself, between the boards and the spine. She opened the book further, bending the joint, and held it up to the light.

Something was in there.

Picking up the nail file, she held the book closer to the light. She shoved the metal tip under whatever was glued inside, pried it loose, and it fell on the nightstand with a clink.

A key. She stared at it. Not anything standard with simple cuts and grooves for the lock in a regular door or to a car. This was smaller than that. Flat. Brass. With unique and intricate toothlike cuts. She'd never seen one like it.

Of course, there was no note telling her what the key was to or what she was supposed to do with it.

Thanks, Dad.

Clearly, her father didn't practice the principle of keeping it simple.

She didn't know what the key might unlock, but Takoda would probably have a good guess.

Swiping the key from the nightstand, she hopped off the bed and went to the door.

Nerves fluttered in her belly and her thighs tingled, all at the thought of seeing him. She hesitated with her hand on the knob.

Being here in Tak's house, sleeping right down the hall from him, the memory of kissing him in the kitchen this morning, was making it impossible for her to continue to pretend.

The butterflies in her tummy, the tingles, the achy, tight feeling that started at her scalp and spread throughout her body, the hot rush of attraction she felt whenever she was in the same room with him. All the visceral physical reactions to him that she was tired of ignoring.

She thought back to the way he'd looked at her in the kitchen. After the kiss. After he told her about the ridiculous promise that he'd made to her brother and intended to keep.

There's a line with you, Kimi, and I can't cross it.

What if she moved the line? Found a way to erase it.

Kimi shoved down her sweatpants and stepped out of them, leaving on the oversized T-shirt with nothing underneath. She tucked the key inside one of the socks she wore and made a decision.

There were plenty of things in the world to be afraid of, and her father had only added more to the list. But when it came to Tak, he was no longer something to fear. Neither was everything he made her feel or want. Not even the possibility of rejection frightened her anymore.

She wanted Takoda Yazzie, and it was up to him to determine what he would do about it. For her, there was no more denying her attraction to him or their chemistry.

No more pretending.

Chapter Eleven

The surveillance footage of the Bitterroot Mountain Hotel the night of the Stracke Group gala showed Thomas running out of the hotel, getting into his two-door, 2002 Ford Bronco, and hightailing down the road. The man with sunglasses was in pursuit.

Within the bounds of bending the rules, Logan had pulled the CCTV footage within a three-mile radius of the hotel for the night Thomas disappeared. Passed it to Takoda.

Sounded like a lot, but in Montana, the CCTV coverage was limited in the largest cities of Billings, Missoula, Great Falls, Bozeman. A drop in the bucket in comparison to some of the most surveilled places in the country like DC or New York. But in Bitterroot Falls and Cutthroat Creek, the number of closed-circuit cameras was sparse, outnumbered by traffic cameras, which were mainly at the busiest intersections.

Takoda had reviewed the footage a dozen times. Both Thomas and the man in pursuit made it beyond the radius of coverage. Only a partial license plate number was visible on the other man's vehicle. A single digit and a letter: 6A. North Dakota plate with the front one not displayed.

Slapping his laptop closed, he cursed the situation. He cursed Thomas Wheeler for endangering Kimi.

And he cursed himself for making the one promise to Jacy he regretted.

But Tak was alive, with a chance for regrets and wants and desires he couldn't slake, while his best friend was buried six feet deep.

"It was supposed to be me," he muttered. "Not you."

Chance had recruited them to join Ironside Protection Services, along with Bo and Eli, all from the RED HORSE Unit. Tak and Jacy had planned their transition from the air force together. To be here in Bitterroot Falls. Close to Kimi. To get her out of trouble when she needed help.

Now, he was following through on the plan for them both.

The knock at his door pulled him from his thoughts.

Kimi.

"Give me a minute." All he had on was a pair of boxer briefs. It was late and he'd hoped she was getting some rest.

He slipped into his jeans, fastened the button and threw on a fitted T-shirt.

A quick glance around to be certain he hadn't left anything embarrassing out, like the photo of her he usually kept tucked away in his wallet. The candid one Jacy had taken the summer before he died.

In the snapshot, Kimi was sitting on a yellow blanket in a field of wildflowers that stretched for miles. The vivid colors of the grass, the flowers, the blanket, her dress, those cowgirl boots she loved so much, contrasted against the backdrop of the snowcapped peaks and the brilliant blue sky. But what had been breathtaking about the photo was her. Kimi in a sexy, purple sundress with thin, delicate straps, her raven hair caught in a soft breeze, her head thrown back in laughter. The 3x5 photo was too small for a frame and a smidge too big to fit his wallet just right. The photo Takoda looked at so often, the edges were crinkled and starting to fade.

Why hadn't Jacy sent a digital version?

Fortunately, he had remembered to put it back in his wallet after he'd stared at it earlier tonight, replaying the mind-blowing kiss they'd shared.

He padded barefoot across the room and opened the door. "Tak."

The sight of Kimi standing in his doorway wearing a T-shirt—an even shorter one than this morning—was too much for his willpower tonight.

Geez, just put him out of his misery right now.

"Anything wrong?" he asked.

"I can't sleep. Mind if we talk for a bit?" She peered up at him, the look on her face so warm, so alluring, so… He couldn't quite pinpoint what he saw in her eyes, but whatever it was, he liked it. A lot.

"Yeah, of course." He went to step out into the hall, but she squeezed by him, pressing her soft body against his as she entered his room.

His heart started racing again.

It was so bizarre how his pulse stayed as steady as a ticking metronome when gunfire and explosions sounded off around him or when he chased down a man who had threatened his loved ones, but the second Kimi touched him, his heart beat double-time, pounding frenetic in his ears.

"Let's go to the living room," he suggested. "I can make you a cup of tea or hot chocolate." Anything to get her out of his bedroom.

Staring at him, she chewed her bottom lip, and for some reason, it was the sexiest thing ever. "No, thanks."

"I'll even light a fire."

Her gaze slid to the fireplace in his room.

Another design decision he thought had been ideal at the time, but he wasn't so sure anymore with Kimi half dressed, standing a few short feet from his bed.

"Light it in here," she said, throwing out the words like a challenge.

"What did you need to talk about?"

She crossed the space separating them and put her palm on his chest. "Have you ever thought about us? Together? Wondered what it would be like if I was yours? And if you were mine?" she asked, and everything inside him tensed and tightened. "Even for one night."

All the time. He couldn't keep her out of his head. The reason none of his relationships lasted was that none of those women could hold a candle to Kimi.

She was so close to him, he felt the soft, feminine heat from her body. Inhaled the scent of honeysuckle in her hair, mixed with the delicate smell of soap on her skin. "Please, don't do this."

"Do what?" Her palm slowly slid up his chest. "We're only having a simple conversation."

Then this conversation was going to test his hold on his less-than-stalwart restraint. Nothing about his deep feelings for her, his desire for her, what he wanted to do with her, was simple.

Backing away, he broke the physical contact between them, but the tension in the room, the electricity in the air, only intensified. He plopped down on his bed and dropped his head into his hands, elbows on his knees. "This is the opposite of simple."

"You make things harder than necessary." She strode over until she was standing in front of him.

He stared down at her sock-covered feet. "Probably."

"I want this. You want this, don't you? So much easier to give in to this thing between us. I don't know, call it chemistry, attraction, whatever. All I know is it's overwhelming when I'm near you, and distracting, invading into my thoughts when I'm not."

"But there's a line," he said, sharp and firm.

"Yeah, yeah, you told me." Kimi stepped in between his legs.

He sat upright to avoid touching her, which had been part of her plan. As soon as he did, she straddled him, sinking down on his lap, her bare thighs pressing against his legs, and wrapped her arms around his neck. He could tell from her eyes, the way her gaze caressed his face, and her light brown cheeks flushed, that her attraction to him was as intense and immediate as his for her. Like radiating from a stoked fire.

"What are you doing?"

"Moving the line." She crushed her lips to his and kissed him.

There was nothing slow or tentative about it, all hunger and urgency, and his brain misfired. She slid her tongue into his mouth, and he groaned, accepting the invasion willingly. Goodness, she knew how to kiss, and he was lost as to why the thought of her doing this with someone else riled him so much.

She rocked her hips against him. Hips that moved in the most aggravating and satisfying way. Before he could process what was happening, his arms were around her and he was kissing her back with all the passion and yearning that had been building inside him.

The sensation of her sweet mouth and her supple body was making him lose his mind. His raunchiest fantasies had nothing on reality. In everything he imagined with her, he often glossed over kissing her. Jumping ahead to the steamy parts where they weren't wearing any clothes. Now he realized that it had been a serious mistake. Colossal.

Her lips on his, their tongues tangling, the way she poured

herself into the kiss while pulling his need to the surface, stoking his craving for her, was the hottest thing he'd ever experienced. That spoke volumes considering he lost track of the number of lovers he'd had throughout the years, some of their faces a blur.

Everything about Kimi caught his blood on fire. Her beautiful face, those finely sculpted features, her silky hair, her soft skin, the way she smelled, how she felt in his arms. This incredible, intelligent woman who brought every cell of his body to life with her touch.

This was hell. Or heaven.

Takoda couldn't be certain. She had him spinning in circles and spiraling out of control. He was losing this battle.

His body tightened, straining with want. He grabbed those soft, undulating hips to either stop her or bring her closer, but he slipped his hand under her shirt. His palm glided over her spine along warm, smooth skin. Then lower to her backside.

Her *bare* backside.

Tak jerked his hands away from her like he'd been scalded and wrenched his mouth to the side. "Kimi," he warned, gritting his teeth against the pure pleasure and sheer torture throbbing through him. "You're not wearing underwear." This test was too great, and he was going to fail. "We agreed."

"We did." The same look she had at his door flashed in her eyes again, and this time he could name it—determination and desire. "But your bedroom isn't a common space."

"I need you to back off." His voice pained, his tone pleading.

"Tell me you don't want me." She trailed a string of kisses across his jaw, down his neck, rocking her hips against him, and he shuddered. "And I will."

He was speechless, unable to lie, unable to utter a single half-truth.

Her lips returned to his, and every reason why she shouldn't be in his arms evaporated. Gone like a wisp of smoke in the wind.

Takoda strained upward, holding her, kissing her harder, plunging his fingers in her hair. He gathered the hem of her T-shirt in his fist to strip it off her, and his doorbell rang.

He stilled, his mouth leaving hers, and she went rigid. His heart was pounding, his breath ragged. Sighing, she dropped her forehead to his shoulder.

The spell was broken. It was a sign. They needed to stop.

The doorbell rang again, three more times, in quick succession. Someone wanted his attention, and it didn't seem as though they were going to leave until they got it.

"I have to answer the door," he said.

"I know." She rolled off to the side, and his body ached at the loss of her on top of him.

Grabbing his Mk 23 from the holster on the floor, he got up and went to see who dared to ring his bell after eleven o'clock at night. After he and the other guys had started working for IPS, they'd each bought a plot of land, not too far from one another. As engineers, they'd designed their homes with the best security features. Privacy film on bullet-resistant windows. External doors made of ballistic steel that could withstand prolonged blunt-force attacks and stop a bullet. Not to mention state-of-the-art security systems with motion-activated lights and security cameras.

He went to the wall-mounted panel near the door. Turned off the alarm. Brought up the camera view of his porch. It was the last person he expected.

Heaving a breath, he opened the front door. "Hey, Dan. What can I do for you?"

Doctor Dan stood with his coat open, showing his green scrubs, his hands stuffed in his pockets. "Is she here?"

"Yeah." Tak stepped aside, letting him in.

Kimi was in the kitchen, standing on the other side of the counter that blocked the lower half of her body.

Tak locked the door and switched on a light in the room. "I'll give you two some privacy."

"No need," DD said. "I won't be staying long."

"What are you doing here?" Kimi asked.

"I went to the hotel, looking for you, but you had checked out. So, I went by your house. I noticed your car parked at your neighbor's. Mr. Simpson told me you were with Takoda. I can't say I'm surprised. I just wish you had been honest with me," he said, his tone scathing.

Talk about awkward. Being privy to their conversation from his bedroom, with the door open, would have been far more comfortable than being quite literally in the middle of it. Tak eased back a bit.

Kimi folded her arms. "I was honest. Always. I know how this looks."

"I thought you didn't need a babysitter."

"I don't. But it turns out I do need a bodyguard."

"So, I was right," the doctor said. "You're not safe. The reason I went looking for you instead of simply calling was because I was worried you might be in some sort of danger. A man snuck into the women's dressing room at the hospital. Broke into your locker. Candace walked in on him. He shoved her into a wall. We had to call the police."

"Oh, my God." Kimi put a hand to her throat. "Is she okay?"

"She will be. No injuries, but she's shaken up. I just wanted to be sure that you're all right." Dan glanced at Tak. "I see you're right where I thought you'd be. At least, I don't have to worry about you anymore." He turned for the door, hesitated, and looked back at her. "Remember when you told me you kissed him." Dan gestured with his head to Tak. "And you couldn't understand why I wasn't upset?"

Kimi's shoulders twitched, as though she were inwardly squirming. "Because you felt a kiss didn't matter. You were just relieved I didn't sleep with him."

Dan shook his head. "That's what you assumed. I had hoped that while we were on a break, you would sleep with him. Satisfy your curiosity and then we could move forward without me wondering when you two would eventually hook up." Dan stared at her, his face hard, his eyes sad. "I mean, he's the reason you broke up with me, isn't it?"

"There were a lot of reasons."

"But he was one of them, at the very top of the list. Right?"

"Yes." She looked away from the doctor. "But what I feel for him goes beyond curiosity," she said to Dan but now looked Takoda straight in the eyes. "It's been much more than that for a long time, but he doesn't feel the same." She cut her gaze back to Dan. "I never would've cheated on you and, just so you know, the number one reason on my list was that we weren't a good fit. I'm sorry if I hurt you."

"I'm not hurt," Dan snapped, his tone defensive. "Only annoyed. I'm a great catch, Kimi. This is your loss. Not mine." He opened the door, hustled down the porch steps and disappeared into the cold darkness.

Taking a deep breath, Takoda locked up and reactivated the alarm. Everything Kimi said was sinking in, seeping in the cracks and crevices inside his chest. Slowly, he strode into the kitchen and approached her. "I do have feelings for you. Strong feelings."

"They're not the same as mine. Not even in the same league. If they were, nothing would stop you from being with me, and I don't mean just some reckless moment where I'm throwing myself at you. One that you could later dismiss and regret." She hiked her chin up at him and shook her head. "I mean, really be with me. Instead, you want to cling to some promise to Jacy. When this was never his intention. I have to believe that. The only thing that should matter between *us*, is any promise you make to me. But it's not because..." Her eyes turned glassy and she shrugged.

There were things she didn't know. About him. About how Jacy died.

"Kimi." He reached for her, but she backed away.

A tear leaked from the corner of her eye and rolled down her cheek. Something painful twisted deep in his gut.

She swiped at her eyes. "I don't want talk about this anymore."

Relief trickled through him at ending this conversation, but he hated leaving things like this. Unsettled. Uneasy.

Her unhappy and on the verge of tears. Because of him.

Not knowing what to do or say, he fell back on the mission. "Tomorrow, we'll work on tracking down Big Billy Burdock and question Peter O'Donnell about the altercation outside the mine. Okay?"

"No, we won't," she said, her voice firm, her shoulders squared. "Logan or one of the other guys will have to do it."

He leaned a hip against the counter. "Why is that?"

"My mom is in Hawaii for two more weeks. Tomorrow, we're going to Spokane to get the necklace. *Together*."

She'd spoken to Aiyana. It would've been nice to know that when she'd knocked on his door.

"Nope," Tak said. "It's a five-hour drive." One way, and a polar vortex was going to hit tomorrow. Driving a long distance in bad weather was enough for him to worry about. He had better check his truck, make sure he had all the essentials. "You can stay at Chance and Winter's place while I go get it." She'd be comfortable and, more importantly, safe on the Lady Luck Ranch. Plenty of armed ranch hands lived on the sprawling property. No one would get to her there while he retrieved the necklace.

Kimi folded her arms. "Only one of us knows the address."

"Simple enough to find with a quick internet search." He could have it in under a minute. Not necessarily a good thing how personal data such as home addresses and phone numbers were easy pickings unless you took steps to protect your privacy.

Thinking it over, the ease with which someone could pull up Aiyana Redbird's address made the trip somewhat risky. Anyone watching him take Interstate 90, heading West, might assume that was where he was headed. They wouldn't even have to tail him either.

"What about where to find the key to the house and the necklace? Or the code to the alarm? Since a Google search won't tell you any of those things, I guess it means we're taking a road trip, together."

Tak heaved a breath. Fighting her on this would be futile. "Fine, you can go, but you've got follow my rules. Nonnegotiable. You do what I say, when I say it, no questions asked, and you've got to wear body armor."

"Are you kidding?" she asked, and he shook his head. "Why do I need body armor?"

"We don't know why these men are after you or how far they're willing to go to get whatever they're after. Desperation can push people to extremes. Then there's the guy with tattoos. He won't hesitate to shoot. *Nonnegotiable*, got it?"

"Okay," she said, raising both palms. "I'll follow the rules."

"We'll leave first thing in the morning." Last time he'd checked the weather, the snowstorm was supposed to hit around late afternoon. They should be able to make it back before the worst of it hit. "Grab the necklace and come straight back. No overnight stay." Though he'd ensure they were prepared for anything. "You should go back to your room and get some sleep."

She slinked forward, drawing closer. "I didn't get a chance to tell you everything I wanted to say."

He assumed they were done with that topic. "It's late. Maybe we shouldn't get back into everything tonight." This was a no-win situation for him. "It's like you want me to prove how I feel about you even if it means breaking my word to your brother." He owed Jacy so much, at the very least, to honor his wishes.

"Generally, that's how a relationship works, Takoda. Two people show each other how they feel. Or it isn't real. But that's not what I'm talking about." Kimi crouched down, pulled something out of her sock and dropped it on the quartz countertop with a *ting*. "I found it in the book my dad gave me. Hidden in the joint along the spine."

"Way to bury the lead earlier." He picked up the key and stared at it. Three words were stamped on it: Do Not Duplicate.

"Any idea what it opens?" she asked.

"A safe-deposit box." This kind of key couldn't be mistaken for anything else. He turned it over. "Number 317." He frowned, thinking it through. "But, of course—"

"We don't know which bank or where?"

"Exactly." Too many possible banks to count and Tak doubted it would be a local one. No telling how far Thomas had driven to open a safe-deposit box.

"There has to be a way to find out."

"Possibly." Tak hoped so. "Since Thomas was being so careful, I don't think he had an automatic monthly payment for the safe-deposit box. I can get Eli to dig into your dad's finances for the last year and see if he made a payment to a bank equal to the amount of a year-long rental fee for a box. But if your dad paid in cash, then there won't be a digital trail."

"I can't shake the sense this is so much bigger than we realize," she said.

"No matter what it is, I'll keep you safe. I'd sooner die than let anything happen to you."

Kimi took a deep breath and shivered. "Which terrifies me. I don't want you to get hurt." She looked away from him. "Why would my dad drag me into the middle of this? Does he care about me at all?"

"Of course, he does. Otherwise, he wouldn't have hired me to protect you."

"Then why didn't he just talk to me when we had lunch? Why all the deception?"

Thomas was a difficult man to understand, but he wasn't cold or ruthless. He was sort of nerdy. Socially awkward. But struck Tak as good-natured. Kindhearted. Wouldn't-hurt-a-fly type of man. Not one who would throw his daughter to the wolves to save himself.

"Maybe he was ashamed. Maybe he hoped things wouldn't come to this." There was a reasonable explanation, one that didn't negate a father's love for his daughter. Perhaps Tak had an idealistic perspective since he imagined his parents had been perfect. His family was loving and protective. Honor meant a great deal to them. All his relationships were framed by those core values. "Don't worry." Tak reached out and caressed her cheek. "We'll keep taking this one step at a time and figure it out. *Together.*"

Kimi gave him a sad, soft smile.

And a hard-hitting punch went straight to his chest, cracking something wide open inside him.

The key was the only solid clue Thomas had left for Kimi. One way or another, they were going to find the bank and the safe-deposit box the key unlocked. They had to.

Chapter Twelve

Thanks to an intensification of the polar vortex, arctic air moved in faster than anticipated. It didn't help that they'd driven directly into it either. Despite the storm coming in early, they had crossed the border into Washington in great time, with no delays on the road.

Takoda had packed the truck as though he were prepping for Armageddon. Blankets. Battery-operated lanterns. Binoculars. An EMT trauma kit. Meals ready to eat. Water. Flares. Bolt cutters. Just-in-case overnight bags. Plus, whatever else he had that she didn't know about. He'd wanted them ready for anything.

That included forcing her to wear a bulletproof vest. Not as bad as she had expected it to be. No thick, clunky, sweltering piece of Kevlar. Under her sweater, she wore a concealable ultrathin body armor T-shirt-style vest. Level IIIA, whatever that meant. Something to do with the type of bullets it stopped. It was flexible and lightweight, allowing her to move freely. He'd also given her a crash course, explaining the differences between soft and hard body armor.

The vest she had on was designed to stop all kinds of handgun rounds while the hard type was heavier and offered more protective power against rifle rounds. The fact he'd insisted she wear one at all meant the man with the tattoos had spooked Takoda Yazzie, and that truly frightened her.

The long, uphill driveway to the house stretched before them as they slowly drove through the layer of snow that had accumulated. Kimi found it relaxing to watch the big, heavy, white flakes fall and dance in the fierce wind, but she wasn't eager to get out of the warm truck.

Davey's and her mom's vehicles were sitting in a single file in front of the attached one-car garage.

Tak stopped behind their cars and threw the gear in Park. "Why doesn't one of them keep their vehicle in the garage?"

"They use it for storage. Holiday stuff. Mom's art supplies. Davey's home brewery."

Glancing around, he left the engine running. "I don't like it. The house is so exposed."

Kimi looked out the window. The trees were set far back from the house, which was situated on a large, cleared plot. The opposite of Tak's place. He'd chosen to build his custom home nestled in the woods on the three-acre parcel of land he'd handpicked, only clearing trees to make way for construction.

The strategic placement wasn't something she had ever considered.

His phone rang. The caller ID popped up on the dashboard. Unknown number.

He tapped an icon on the screen, taking the call. "Takoda Yazzie."

"This is Orson. Chance gave me your number last night. He thought it would be faster to contact you directly when I found something."

Kimi and Tak exchanged a look. Hope welled in her chest. They needed a break.

"I take it you did."

"Yes," Orson said, "and *not yet*."

Interesting way of phrasing it, Kimi thought.

"I'm in my truck," Tak said. "I'd rather not talk here. Let me get inside."

"Two minutes. I'll call back."

"Make it ten," Tak said.

"Ten it is." Orson hung up.

Tak shut off the engine and put on his jacket, leaving it unzipped. Setting his cowboy hat firmly on his head, he turned toward her. "Hang back a second," he said, putting a palm on her arm and giving her a hard stare.

Her belly quivered under the heat of that steady gaze. When he looked at her like that, the only thing she could think about was how it would feel to have his hands all over her.

If she loved him—and she was *in love* with him—wasn't she entitled to at least one night in his arms? One night he wouldn't look back on with regret.

Tak hopped out of the truck, shutting the door. He took the binoculars from his jacket pocket and walked around, scanning the area.

Waiting for him, Kimi slipped on her winter gear—knit hat, down-filled parka, gloves—and tugged the hood of her coat over her head. A few minutes later, Takoda appeared outside the passenger-side door, squinting against the pelting snow.

He opened the door for her, letting in a biting rush of wind. Kimi climbed out of the truck, set her foot on the running board and slipped. She might have fallen out of the truck if not for Tak catching her, wrapping his arm around her and setting her down.

"Oh, thanks." With her palm on his solid chest, she glanced up at his handsome face and laughed off the instant heat the close contact made flare.

He grinned. "You okay?"

She nodded. "Yeah. Clumsy of me."

Keeping his arm around her, he shouldered the door shut and tried to shield her from the whipping wind and fierce fall of flurries as they trudged the rest of the way up the long driveway.

"Aren't you freezing with your coat open?" she asked.

"I want to be able to draw my weapon quickly if the need arises. A little cold for a couple of minutes won't kill me."

"No, but it might give you pneumonia."

Another grin that had her using the wind as an excuse to snuggle closer.

They crossed the yard to get around to the front door.

"The key is under that flowerpot," Kimi said, pointing to the largest one that was painted blue.

He lifted it and grabbed the key. "Not the best hiding spot." He unlocked the door, held it open, ushering her inside, and closed it with the next gust.

The alarm beeped, thirty seconds of warning to let the homeowner disarm the system.

Out of the freezing cold, she stomped her feet and shoved her hood back before stepping farther into the house. She went to the security panel and entered the code, and the beeping stopped.

"Let's get what we came for," he said. "Where is the necklace?"

Tugging off her gloves, she led the way through the house. It had a large, open floor plan, with the bedrooms at the back. They passed the dining space with its oversize sliding-glass doors overlooking the valley. She understood why her mother loved being out there. The place was a rare gem. Beautiful and peaceful.

Though to her, she preferred Takoda's house and view. His land felt different. Sunrises and sunsets were the best. He'd picked a great spot. No matter the season, it was a picture-perfect postcard of a slice of heaven.

Since the last time she'd been in Spokane, Davey had given her mom free rein to redecorate. It looked like a completely different house. New furniture and curtains, fresh coat of paint. Artistic touches of Aiyana Redbird hung on almost every wall. Her mother had a special gift to be able to touch a person's soul with her paintings. The great Thomas Wheeler, with his magical sixth sense, could find palladium. Even Jacy had been gifted. Her brother could build anything.

Kimi always wondered if she had a gift. On the rodeo circuit, she'd recognized she had a little talent and a lot of luck. Maybe it was healing people. Jacy inspired her to become a nurse, but a career in medicine felt like her true calling.

In the primary bedroom, she went to the dresser and turned on a floor lamp beside it. Opening the top-right drawer, she found the jewelry case exactly where her mom said it would be. The necklace was in a velvet-lined section of the box. She held it up by the chain and the oblong pendant dangled. Fine silver glinted in the light from the lamp, and she looked over the intricate, colorful etching of a butterfly. No denying it was pretty.

The phone rang. Unknown number again. Orson.

Takoda set the cell on the dresser and put the call on speaker. "What do you have?" he asked, taking the necklace from her.

"The photos of both persons of interest you guys sent were pretty worthless. The sunglasses covered most of one guy's face. Since you said that he's been spotted over the past several days, I tapped into the surveillance footage of the local gas stations. Not many between Bitterroot Falls and Cutthroat Creek. Cross-referenced his image with one you gave me of his vehicle. Found him. Of course. Everyone goes to a fueling station eventually and they all have cameras. His name is Fred Foley. He works for Red Sentry Stronghold."

Takoda stopped examining the pendant, his brow furrowing. "The private security firm?"

"Yep. His vehicle is registered to them as well."

"Then someone must've hired him," Kimi said.

"There's another person on the line?" Orson asked.

"Yes, sorry," Tak said. "Kimi Wheeler. She's the woman I was hired to protect. It's just the two of us."

"Next time, state if the call isn't private at the beginning," Orson said, his tone sharp with irritation. "I breached Red Sentry's firewall. Didn't take much effort. I would *not* recommend their services. Anyway, Red Sentry assigned Foley to work for a shell corporation. While I was in their system, I noticed he's not the only one. Steve Higgins is also on the same contract."

"I was attacked by two men in Kimi's house. Now we know who the second guy is." Tak fiddled with the pendant, a dull *snick* sounded and a hidden mini flash drive slid out.

They exchanged a quick glance.

"Any luck finding out who owns the shell corporation?" Takoda asked.

Orson went into explaining shell corporations, dummy companies, and the layers of protection.

On a closer look of the flash drive, she noticed it wasn't a regular USB but a Type-C—the kind you could pop into an android phone.

What on earth had her father put on it?

"The owner has taken several clever steps to hide their identity," Orson said. "But I got a name for you. Bill Burdock."

"The loan shark?" Kimi wondered aloud.

With a similar puzzled expression, Tak slipped the flash

drive back into its hiding place and handed it to her. She tucked it away in the pocket of her jeans.

"Since Red Sentry is based in North Dakota and these fellas are out-of-towners," Orson said, "I took the liberty of finding out where they were staying. You're welcome. First, they were checked in at the Goldeneye Inn off Route 93, just outside of town. The inn looks like a dump, but then they upgraded big-time to the Bitterroot Mountain Hotel two nights ago."

Goose bumps erupted over her skin. "They knew I was staying at the BMH. What would've happened if you didn't bring me to your house?"

Tak put a hand on her forearm, and his touch calmed her fear.

"Thanks, Orson," Tak said. "At least with some names, we know who we're looking for and can get the cops to pick them up."

Logan was free and clear to bring in Foley and charge him for mugging her. Too bad they couldn't prove that Higgins had broken into her house, but surely Logan had enough to question him. "What about the third guy?" she asked. "The one with the tattoos."

Orson whistled. "Talk about tricky. None of the photos that you guys sent had a good shot of his face. Running through my regular facial recognition program wouldn't have worked. So, I had to get creative. You all stated you had never seen him before. I figured he was from out of town also and had to sleep somewhere. The Goldeneye and Bitterroot Mountain Hotel were a bust. The next closest place was Lariat Suites. Hacked their front desk camera and bingo. He checked in yesterday morning. Rented a black Lincoln Navigator from the Missoula airport."

"The first day this guy is in town, finding me is at the top of his list of things to do?" Find her? Question her?

Hurt her?

"I think it was about simply finding you," Tak said. "He was scoping out the group. Seeing what he was dealing with. Just one bodyguard or several." Takoda scrubbed his hand over the scruff on his jaw. "Orson, please tell me this means you have a name for this guy."

"Now we've reached the *not yet* part I mentioned earlier. The thing is, I dug up five different names with licenses and passports for him. All aliases. Names of dead people. His true identity is unknown for now. This guy is a ghost."

Kimi stared at Tak. His brow wrinkled with worry.

"What does that mean exactly?" she asked with a sinking sensation in the pit of her stomach.

"It could mean a couple of different things. He has a powerful friend somewhere, looking out for him. Or…" the hacker said, dragging out the word and the suspense, "he did an excellent job of erasing his identity at a very early age. But if he's an active professional, like you suspect, then someone knows about him. In either case, the next best place for me to look is in the dark folders of government agencies. FBI, Homeland Security, CIA. See if I can get a hit on him with the better photos I have from the motel. I've cracked some of their systems before, but I'm talking years ago. Don't get me wrong, I can do it again. The trick is doing it without getting caught. They've wised up and are smart enough to lay traps for people like me who can get through. May take longer than you like. But it'll be double my original fee to do it."

Kimi shook her head. *Too much money*, she mouthed.

"Give us a minute," Tak said. He muted the call. "It's worth it to know who we're dealing with. Right now, whoever this guy is, this ghost has us at a disadvantage. I don't want you to worry about the expense. If Chance won't cover the cost from IPS funds, then I'll pay the bill."

Part of her wanted to hug him for his generosity. A more practical part of her wasn't sure it was the best way to proceed. "It's a lot of money." They had already burned through the retainer, plus used IPS funds. Orson was expensive. Thorough and fast and worth it, but expensive. "There's also risk to Orson by hacking into government sites. Knowing the name of this ghost won't tell us who he's working for or minimize any threat he might pose." Shaking her head, she remembered something Bo had said last night at dinner. "It doesn't change the landscape of what we're dealing with." A dangerous man. Knowing his name wouldn't make a difference. "I say, let's focus on Burdock. See if Logan or IPS can find him and tell us what is going on."

She could tell by his grimace that he didn't like it, but he nodded.

Tak took the call off mute. "Orson, we're going to hold off. For now. If we change our minds and decide we need you to press forward, we'll let you know."

"No problem. Here's my number." The hacker passed it along and Tak programmed into his phone. "Remember, it will take time, and I'll need my fee wired in advance."

"All right. Understood. Thanks." Takoda ended the call. "I want to get out of here and on the road." He turned off the lamp and peeked through the curtain out the window. "It's really starting to come down. You can see what's on the flash drive after we hit the interstate."

As they walked back through the house, Tak's head swiveled as he looked out every window they passed. Near the front door, he pulled a curtain back and looked around outside while she set the alarm. The security system began the one-minute countdown before it was activated.

He stepped outside first. Kimi pulled on her gloves, crossed the threshold, and shut the door. A blast of snow whooshed over her.

She locked it. “Ready?” she asked, pointing to the heavy flowerpot so he could lift it and she could replace the key.

He held up a fisted hand, instructing her to hold in place and be quiet. A military gesture she had seen enough times in movies to understand its meaning.

Takoda scanned the area, and she hoped it was out of an abundance of caution, and not because anything was actually wrong.

How much and how far could he see with the awful wind blowing the heavy snowfall, obscuring their vision a few hundred feet from the house?

Time stretched, each second that ticked by an agonizing eternity as she shivered in the cold. Finally, he lowered his hand and lifted the flowerpot.

“What was it?” She set the key down on the perfect, snow-free circle of concrete.

“Not sure.” He put the pot down. “I had a feeling, not sure how to explain it. And with the wind, I can’t see if there are any other footprints in the snow besides ours.” Slipping an arm around her, he ushered her off the stoop. “Just being careful.”

She shoved her gloved hands into her pockets and was about to take a breath of relief when he glanced back over his shoulder and then urged her to hurry across the yard.

A shiver rushed down her spine, like the icy fingers of a ghost. “What’s wrong?” she asked over the howl of the wind, anxiously trying to look behind them.

In response, he drew his weapon and shoved her forward ahead of him.

It was the only warning she received before he yelled, “Run!”

A clap of thunder cracked through the roar of wind and one of the flowerpots on the stoop exploded.

Not thunder. The boom was a gunshot.

Gunfire kicked up snow around them, bright muzzle flashes erupting through the snowy haze.

She bolted across the yard, heading for the driveway, praying she didn’t slip. Snapping a fast look over her shoulder, she spotted them. Two muscular men in black had emerged from around the other side of the house, bounding through the snow. One she recognized—her shadow with sunglasses, Fred Foley. The other guy must’ve been Steve Higgins.

Takoda fired back, the shockingly loud sound of his weapon, so much closer to her, splitting the air. She made it to the driveway and raced down the slick pavement.

Gunfire pinged off metal, sparks flaring in the swirling gusts of snow. She screamed. Cringing, she ran, trying to make herself as small a target as possible, covering the back of her head with her hands. Her breath caught in her lungs, jammed there as she braced for the shattering sound of more gunshots.

Bullets slammed into the side of Davey’s car, setting off the alarm. Her mom’s headlight burst. The muscles in Kimi’s stomach tensed until she felt sick.

Fear coiled in her chest, throbbing behind her sternum, but not for herself. *Tak, please be okay. Please.*

Looking over her shoulder, she saw Takoda. He was on his feet, hustling in her direction as he fired back at the two men.

“Don’t stop!” Takoda called out.

Kimi didn’t need to be told twice. More shots came in quick succession. She scrambled along the driveway. Her heart knocked against her ribs as she approached the truck.

She hit an icy patch and slipped. Throwing her arms out to her sides, she regained her balance. Pressed on. Didn't slow down.

A buzzing came from behind her, grew louder and louder, and then swooped right over her head. Kimi glanced up into the falling snow. A drone streaked past her and then flew higher, ascending, circling back toward the gunfire.

The truck's lights flashed on, the engine starting remotely with a satisfying grumble. She hurried around the front of the truck, to the passenger-side door, flung it open, and climbed inside. Slamming the door closed, she watched Takoda shooting back.

One man in black dropped, but he was still moving, crawling through the snow.

Tak raced to the truck and hopped in behind the wheel. Everything inside her released. He jerked the gear into Reverse and sped down the driveway. Snow kicked up around them, spitting into the air.

Tak put a hand on her shoulder and shoved her head down behind the dashboard. Once the rear tires hit the street, the rear end of the truck fishtailed in the snow with a screech. He slammed the pickup into Drive, stomped on the accelerator and zoomed down the street.

He checked the rearview and side mirrors, but something caught his attention outside her window and then he swore.

"What now?" she asked, staring up at him, crouched in an awkward position.

"I just spotted a black Lincoln Navigator parked on the other street at a higher elevation. It has a view of Davey's property."

"The ghost?"

He shook his head. "I can't be sure. I only caught a glimpse of the vehicle."

"The drone."

"Drone? What drone?"

"There was a drone that flew right over my head. Someone had to be operating it. Sure wasn't the guys shooting at us."

Takoda swore again.

"Is it safe? Are they following us?"

He checked the mirrors once more. "I think we're okay. I shot one of them. Probably slowing them down. If the ghost was out there, too, then he'll make time to get the drone before following us." He shifted in his seat and groaned.

As she glanced over at him, she noticed his arm. His sleeve had a hole and there was blood.

Panic threatened to squeeze the air from her lungs. She forced herself to breathe. "You're bleeding."

"I'm aware. Consequence of being shot."

"We need to pull over." She scanned the street for a spot where they could stop. "I have to check you."

His gaze bounced up to the rearview mirror. "No. I want to make that light," he said, pointing at the traffic signal.

Reluctantly, she nodded as he stomped on the gas, racing through a yellow light that was turning red, and made a hard left onto the access road that would eventually lead out of town.

"Tak—"

"No! We can't stop. They found us. Even though I was laser focused on ensuring we didn't have a tail on our way here. But they still popped up. Must have spotted us taking I-90 and pieced it together. We can't stop. Not yet. Not until we're a good distance away and I know you're safe. I'll be fine." He gave her a calm, reassuring glance that did little to quell her growing worry for him.

Chapter Thirteen

Pushing the speed limit as much as he dared on I-90 East, Takoda focused on the road, keeping his grip steady on the wheel despite the excruciating pain in his arm and situational awareness vigilant.

No tail.

Not that they needed to follow close behind them if those men thought they would be headed back home.

"You're losing blood," Kimi said, her voice calm. "I need to check the wound."

"Not yet." She'd already been exposed to crossfire back at the house. His injury would have to wait.

"The storm is getting worse. We have to stop anyway. Driving through it with you injured is nuts. We need to find somewhere I can examine you and we can ride out the blizzard until it's over," she said, but he didn't respond. "Tak!"

She was right. He would be useless to her if the bullet had hit an artery and he passed out from blood loss.

"Okay." They would cross the state line into Idaho within minutes. "It has to be in a large city. It'll make it harder for anyone to find us." They'd reach Post Falls first, but he'd prefer one that was bigger. "We'll head to Coeur d'Alene. On your phone do a Google search. Look for a hotel, but not right off the freeway. And we need a parking garage close to it. In case they search the lots of the hotels, they won't see my truck parked there. Probably faster if you pinpointed the garages first."

Nodding, she said, "Got it." She took her phone from her coat pocket. It didn't take her long. "I found something. A city parking garage in the heart of Coeur d'Alene near the lake. There's an inn about a five-minute walk away."

Five minutes in this weather with a gunshot wound, hauling supplies, would feel like fifty. But they had no choice. "All right."

The adrenaline pumping through him cooled and the pain in his arm bloomed as they drove sixteen minutes, a little less than fourteen miles, before she directed him to get off the interstate.

"Take exit 13," she said, and he did. "At the bottom of the off-ramp, make a right."

He followed her directions to the garage and parked on the second level even though there were spots on the first. Gritting his teeth against the pain, he grabbed the EMT kit housed in a discreet black backpack. Then he stuffed a couple of MREs and water in one of the overnight bags and locked the truck.

"Give me the pack," she said.

"No, I've got it."

"This isn't the time to be chivalrous. You're hurt. I can carry the kit on my back with no problem since I wasn't shot in the arm and can hold one of the overnight bags. That'll free you up to cover us if necessary." She held out her hand, eyes gleaming with a resolve that wouldn't take *no* for a response.

Her insistence to help him meant more than he cared to admit.

Not wanting to push himself until he knew how bad his injury was, he swallowed his pride and let her take the trauma kit.

She slid her arms through the straps, putting the pack on

her back, and took the lighter overnight bag. Snaking one of her arms around his waist, she held on tightly to him.

"Nothing wrong with my legs, you know."

Her only response was to roll her eyes.

The cold, biting wind ripped through him as they trekked the quarter mile through the snow to the Arrow Point Inn.

He took money out of his pocket and stuffed the bills in her hand. "When we get inside, you go to the front desk and get us a room. I'll hang back," Tak said, and she glanced at his bullet hole and blood on his jacket. "Pay in cash and register under a fake name so we can't be tracked." The way things had escalated back at the house, turning into a shootout, he didn't want those men to know where to find her.

"Got it."

Inside the warm entrance, he took the overnight bag from her and headed to the sitting room adjacent to the foyer while she strode up to the front desk. Takoda kept Kimi and the front door in his sights. An older man at the desk was all smiles as he chatted with her, only glancing over once in the direction of the sitting room. Tak tipped his Stetson in greeting and the white-haired man appeared satisfied.

Six minutes later, Tak met her at the staircase.

She held up the key to room twelve. "Come on. Second floor."

They headed up the steps.

"Did he ask why I didn't check in with you?"

"Before he could, I told him you were in a bad mood." She removed her hat and gloves. "Triple whammy of the snowstorm hitting early, low blood sugar, and that we had a fight. He was very sympathetic."

"As beautiful as you are, I'm sure he was."

She grinned at him.

He followed her to the last door at the end of the hall and stared at the placard. "The bridal suite?"

"The place is empty. Off season and the storm. And I did say he was sympathetic."

She unlocked the door. They stepped inside the large room and dropped their bags.

The four-poster, king-size bed dominated the space. He looked around. Outdated wallpaper. Original hardwood floors. Floral designs on the area rug and comforter fabric. Adjoining bathroom. Gas fireplace. A small bistro-style table for two with chairs was tucked in a corner near a window and the fireplace.

They could've done much worse.

"A little chilly in here," she said, rubbing her hands together.

He set his hat on a nightstand. "Since the place is empty, they probably have the temp set low to save on the heating bill."

After she took off her coat, she started the fire. "It should warm up in here relatively quickly." She pulled her sweater over her head and quickly stripped off the body armor vest, leaving her in a tank top and bra. A sigh of relief slipped from her lips and she stretched. Kimi came over to him and helped him ease his jacket off. She studied the jacket sleeve. "There's no exit hole. The bullet is still in your arm."

Meant she'd have to dig it out. It was going to hurt like hell.

"We can go to the hospital," she offered. "When I was looking for a place for us to stay, I found one. Twelve-minute drive from here."

"Plus, there's the time it'll take to get the truck and the wait to be seen. We both know a gunshot wound has to be reported to the police. Unwanted attention we don't need. You can take care of it."

"I can, but I only mention it because there won't be any anesthetic in the kit."

At least she didn't offend him by asking the question that was clearly on her mind.

"Don't worry about me. I can handle the pain."

Pursing her lips, she riffled through her purse and took out an elastic hair tie. Gathering her hair up, she put it in a messy bun and secured it with the black band. She grabbed the med kit and put a hand on his lower back, steering him into the bathroom.

Lowering the toilet seat lid, she said, "You know the drill."

He sat, eager to get it over with.

Kimi handed him a packet of pain reliever tablets and a bottle of water.

While he popped the pills and washed them down, she laid out supplies on the counter and tugged on latex gloves. Turning to him, she unbuttoned his flannel shirt.

"I've got it," he snapped.

She slapped his hand away and peeled the shirt off carefully. Underneath, he wore a long-sleeved compression thermal that fit him like a second skin. "I'm going to have to cut it off." Crouching down, she rummaged through the bag. "Great. No scissors."

He unsheathed his MAMU knife he had secured at his waist, flipped it in the air, catching it by the blade, and offered her the handle. "Be careful. It's very sharp."

Taking it, she smiled, and as usual, the sight left him breathless.

She plucked the material away from his skin and sliced. The knife slashed through the shirt with ease. She did the same with the back. As she slowly peeled off the sleeve from his injured arm, he gave the other side a simple tug and it fell.

Leaning over, she inspected the wound. His skin prickled with warmth at her proximity.

"The good news is the bullet isn't near your brachial artery. I'll remove it and then clean the wound. Take off your pants."

What? "Why?"

"It's going to bleed. A lot. It'll ruin your jeans."

Nodding, he said, "Okay." Deep down, he wondered if it was a bad idea. Having on fewer clothes around her was never good.

"Right now, I'm in nurse mode. Chop. Chop." She clapped her hands, snapping him into action.

Kicking off his boots, he unzipped his jeans and stripped out of them. With only his boxer briefs and socks left, he sat back down.

Her gaze raked over him, landing on the holstered Ruger strapped to his ankle before bouncing back up to his face. The entire time her expression read *pure professional.*

Grabbing a towel, she draped it over his lap. She opened the packaging of the sterilized forceps. "Can't rush this. I'll need to go slowly. It's better if we don't stop once we get started and get it done."

"Go ahead. Just do it."

"Here we go." She shifted his arm toward the light, peered closer, and stuck the forceps in the wound.

Agony flared white-hot. Shutting his eyes, he gritted his teeth and focused on breathing. As she dug around, trying to get a hold on the bullet, the pain splintered and bloomed. He clutched his knee, went somewhere else in his mind. Heard the ocean, felt the warmth of the sun and grains of sand beneath his feet, saw Kimi on the beach, smiling at him. Holding his hand. Stroking his face. Calling his name.

"Takoda, I got it."

He opened his eyes to see her holding the bullet with the forceps.

"It's all in one piece," she said, dropping the bloody slug in the trash and the forceps in the sink. Blood poured from his wound and she pressed a piece of gauze to it. "Ready to irrigate it?" She grabbed the saline solution.

"There should be hydrogen peroxide in the kit."

"Saline is better. Hydrogen peroxide can damage the skin, and it'll only delay healing. Trust me, I know what I'm doing."

"Sorry. You're the expert," he said. "You know, Jacy always thought medicine was your calling. I think he was right."

Her brow wrinkled in doubt. "Really?"

"Yeah. He said you had healing hands. After you breezed through your degree and I saw how much you loved being a nurse, I thought you'd go on to med school. Become a doctor."

Something flashed across her face as she held his gaze, and then it was gone. "Brace yourself."

Freezing-cold saline blasted into the wound.

"Geez!" Clenching his jaw, he fisted a hand. "That hurt worse than taking out the bullet."

She dabbed at the blood leaking from the hole in his arm. "Stitches won't be possible. These kits don't usually come with sutures." She held up a skin stapler. "Breathe through it."

He nodded. Instead of shutting his eyes this time, he stared at her face while she worked.

Kimi held the sides of the wound together and pressed in the first staple.

A sharp pang arced through him and he ground his teeth. Found his center as he looked at her, memorizing every detail. Her smooth, light brown skin. The way the light hit her, bringing out the hints of brown in her hair and flecks of copper in her eyes. The sultry curve of her lips. How intently she focused. The steadiness of her hands.

She was so beautiful it made his heart ache.

"All done," Kimi said.

He looked at the three staples in his arm. Barely felt the last two.

She wet a washcloth with warm water, cleaned the blood from him, stroking his skin with such tender care, and leveled that bright brown gaze on his face. He fought a rush of need, a familiar struggle, but found it hard to suppress. It was then he realized this attraction, this desire, had been seeping into the cracks and fissures of his armor like the water that freezes inside a rock, expanding and breaking it apart.

Lowering his head, he was at a loss, his restraint so close to shattering.

"Just in case," she said, placing a hemostatic dressing over the wound with adhesive. "It'll prevent any further bleeding."

"You did a great job. Thank you."

"Anything for you." She gave him a quick kiss on the lips.

Surprised, pleasantly, he stilled. "Please, don't tell me you give all your patients kisses."

"Why? Would it make you jealous?"

"Yes." The word slipped from his mouth without thinking.

Grinning, she plucked off her gloves. "Well, I'm all out of lollipops." She kissed him again. "So lucky you."

A knock sounded at the door.

Tak grabbed his gun from the holster on the floor and was on his feet.

Kimi put a hand on his chest. "Relax. It's only Jim. He offered to bring up some chili to get your blood sugar up. He didn't want me to have to deal with Mr. Grumpy Pants in the bridal suite."

Narrowing his eyes, he followed her to the door. "We have MREs."

"Ugh. That's not real food."

"May not be good, but I guarantee it's real." He checked through the peephole, verified it was the older man from the front desk and no one else was in the hall. Then he nodded.

She opened the door and he stayed behind it, gun in his hand. "Thank you so much, Jim. This is really kind of you."

"The sooner you can get your husband in a good mood, the better. This is a family recipe sure to please the pickiest eater. Enjoy your night, nuzzled up close in the best room in the house."

Kimi stepped back, holding a tray of food. Two bowls of chili covered with plastic wrap, bread rolls, a bottle of sparkling apple cider and two mugs.

Tak shut the door. "Husband, huh?"

She shrugged. "I told him we were married. Anne and Guy Drury."

"Guy? Very original. Whatever story you spun certainly worked to win him over."

She set the food on the table. "I was convincing when I spoke about you being my husband." Looking up at him, she flattened her hands on his bare chest. Skimmed her fingers back and forth over his skin.

His insides churned with need. "What exactly did you say?"

"That we were newlyweds." Her hand slid up to the base of his neck. "And we were coming from my mom's house." Her thumb slid over his chin and jaw.

Each gentle stroke was driving him wild. "And?"

"There was a fight. An ugly one. And for a few frightening moments, I thought about what it would be like to lose you." Tears glistened in her eyes, and his heart squeezed. "It would kill me, Takoda." She stepped closer, bringing their bodies flush. "One of us, both of us, could've died today. I don't want either of us to leave this world without knowing what it's like for us to be together. But with no regrets."

Risking his life, facing death, never bothered him. Not until Kimi. His existence was punctuated the day he'd met her, everything redefined—there was simply before Kimi and after Kimi. She was the reason he wanted to plant roots in Montana. In Bitterroot Falls. To be near her. It was impossible for him to say when he'd fallen in love with her. The only thing he knew for certain was that every day he wasn't with Kimi, he felt a stab of hunger for her and found nourishment at the very sight of her.

He wanted her and not for one night. A lifetime with her wouldn't be enough.

Wrapping his arms around her warm body, he cupped her face in his hand and let go of every good argument about why he should stay away from her.

Awareness, attraction, need—something electric vibrated in the air and licked over his skin. She rose on the balls of her feet, bringing his mouth to hers, and the last bit of control holding him back crumbled. All his rules, the promises he'd made to everyone else, faded away.

Tak inhaled her scent, drawing her closer. She kissed him harder, deeper, while her hands went exploring. Lifting a leg, she caught it behind his knee. Rubbed and writhed her body against him, luring him in and turning him on like no one else.

She drew one palm slowly down between them, slipping a hand in his boxer briefs and cupping him. "You were shot, had the slug removed without any anesthetic, the wound stapled, and you're still *up*."

"I've never been so up in my life."

She squeezed, and he groaned. "You like my touch?"

"You have no idea what that does to me. What you do to

me." He kissed her, taking possession of her mouth, running his hand over the curves of her body. Heat overwhelmed him. Easing his lips from hers, he caressed her face. "I want you. This. Us." He met her gaze, and she smiled, lighting up parts of him that he didn't even realize existed. "No regrets," he vowed.

Chapter Fourteen

The bubble of euphoria gradually leveled off in the afterglow. Kimi nestled her head on Takoda's chest. His good arm was wrapped around her, holding her close as they lay in bed, their legs tangled. Every muscle in her body was relaxed. She'd had sex before, but this was the first time she'd ever made love. Experienced something so deep, it moved her heart. Touched her soul. Made her want to connect in every way possible to another.

To him.

Tak played in her hair and brushed his lips across her forehead. "How do you feel?"

"Relieved." Finally, he'd made love to her, and he wasn't running away from her afterward. They were going to do this. Be together or try to, anyway. "And happy." Which was strange, considering everything else going on. "But I should be asking you that." She leaned up on her elbow and looked down at him. "How's your arm?"

"Sore, but it'll be fine."

"You should ice it. There was an instant cool pack in the kit." She went to get up, but he tightened his grip on her.

"Later. I don't want to ice it now."

"Then what do you want?"

He cupped her breast and kissed her. "I'll give you three guesses."

She smiled. Reaching over him, she grabbed his wallet from the nightstand that he'd put there before they had gotten too far earlier without using protection. "Let's see if you have any more condoms." Apparently, he had some on him at all times. *Wildfire through dry brush.* Well, not anymore. Now, he was hers. Opening his billfold, she noticed a photograph hidden inside. "What's this?"

"Don't look at that," he said, trying to take it from her.

Sitting up, she leaned away from him. "Carrying around a picture of an old girlfriend?" Jealousy spiked through her and she instantly wanted to burn it. Kimi pulled out the photo and shock washed over. It was of her…when she'd had a picnic with Jacy. Their last picnic together. "Why didn't you want me to see it?"

He sat up and shrugged. "It's embarrassing. That I've been carrying your picture around for years. Looking at it, at you, way more than I'll ever admit."

Her heart ballooned to near bursting. All this time, he'd had a thing for her, and she hadn't realized. "How did you get this?"

"Jacy sent it to me. With a note that simply said I had *missed out on the best day*."

She smiled. "It had been a great day. Perfect weather. Warm and balmy. The only thing missing was you," she said, thinking back on it. "Funny thing is, when he took this picture, we were talking about you. Jacy was trying to convince me to leave the rodeo circuit. Stay home. Go into medicine. I said, *Marry Takoda and have a few kids*. Pretended to be joking, and I laughed. That's when he snapped the photo. But I was secretly serious. A fantasy I didn't think would ever be reality because you never showed the slightest interest in me. And do you know what Jacy told me?"

"Stay away from me?"

"No. He told me I could do a lot worse than you. That you were a good man, the best guy he'd ever known, and he couldn't think of anyone else he'd rather have as a brother. I thought that was his way of giving me his blessing."

It is time. Jacy's voice in her head was clear but faint. *Time for me to stop standing in the way.*

Kimi smiled, hoping it really was her brother talking to her, telling her he thought this was right. "I had planned to test the waters with you when you got back from the deployment, but then…"

"Jacy died."

She nodded. "I just don't understand why he would make you promise not to be with me when he was giving me the green light. At least, I thought he was." It still made no sense. "When did he ask you to give your word not to touch me?"

"After I first met you and he saw the way I looked at you."

"What?" she said in disbelief. That was a lifetime ago. "I was barely a woman, running wild, looking for trouble. Jacy had been right, back then, to keep us apart." Neither of them had been ready for anything serious. Takoda had still had lots of wild oats to sow, and she'd needed to figure out who she was, what she wanted. "Jacy didn't send you a photo of me and him, the two of us together. I think he sent you this picture of just me as his way of releasing you from your promise." They had both grown and matured and understood what was at stake.

"A part of me felt like he was teasing me. Taunting me with that picture of you, looking so sexy. So beautiful. Which would've been cruel. Jacy was never cruel. I should've known better. Your theory makes more sense."

"Yes, it does." She leaned in and kissed him. "And you don't have any more condoms."

Squeezing his eyes closed, he groaned.

Kimi figured she'd torture him for a couple of hours before letting him know she had an emergency stash in her purse.

"Hey, um, we need to talk." He shifted in the bed, angling toward her, and took her hand in his. "There's something I need to tell you." His expression turned serious.

Taking a deep breath, she prepared herself. As long as he didn't have a secret wife somewhere, whatever he needed to tell her, she could handle it. "What is it?"

"It's about Jacy."

He hesitated. A long time.

So long, she flattened her hand on his chest. His heart thudded against her palm. She would've sworn the look on his face was fear mixed with sadness. But whatever made him afraid, scared her, too. "Please, just spit it out."

"You don't know everything about his death," he said, his tone grim.

She tensed. "The air force hardly told us anything at all because it was classified."

"Yeah, um, I can't tell you everything, but I can tell you what I should've four years ago. We were supporting a spec op mission in Syria. The day it happened, we were building a bridge. One of us needed to keep watch while the rest of the team worked on construction. We drew straws. It was supposed to be Jacy." His voice hollowed. "But I'd hurt my ankle on our HALO jump into the target area."

Jacy and Tak had told her enough for her to understand the dangers of a HALO jump. The parachute had to be opened at a low altitude after free-falling for a period of time. It required a special military oxygen delivery system. They'd pointed out an example to her once in a scene in a Tom Cruise film.

"Your brother wanted me to swap places with him. He said I should take point and secure the perimeter. Since I was a better shot, and with my bad ankle, I agreed to do it.

Everything was clear. For a while. They were almost done when armed insurgents snuck up on our position. I… I took out as many of them as I could, but one slipped past me. Got through." Tak lowered his head. "The guy had explosives. Blew the bridge." His voice strained, cracking. "Jacy didn't make it out. Because of me. I failed to keep him safe. Jacy and one other guy died. On my watch."

The details, the words, the description of how she'd lost her brother sank in. Then the devastation on Tak's face hit her.

"Takoda," she whispered, pressing a palm to his cheek. When he lifted his head and met her eyes, there was so much unspeakable sorrow in them, it broke her heart into a hundred sympathetic pieces. Tears she hadn't realized were building fell, rolling down her cheek. "It wasn't your fault."

"But it was. I let him down. He should've been the one protecting the perimeter. I was supposed to help build the bridge. It should've been me who died that day. Not him."

Throwing her arms around his neck, she drew him into a tight hug. "Stop. It isn't true. You two had a dangerous job. Part of what made you both heroes was how you accepted the risks, knowingly putting your lives on the line for this country. I loved Jacy, and I miss him every day. So much so, that sometimes I swear I can hear him talking to me."

Tak eased back and looked at her with tears in his eyes. "Yeah? Me, too."

"I know he loved you and would've traded his life for yours. Without hesitation. You did the best you could."

"My best wasn't good enough."

"How many others survived?"

"Seven."

"You have to remember the ones you saved." More tears fell as she kissed him. "I can't believe you've lived with the weight of this on your own." For four years. "Jacy would've wanted you to make it. To live without carrying around guilt or survivor's remorse. So that you could be here. With me."

Pulling him down to the bed, she hugged him, holding him in her arms, stroking his head. Showing him how much she loved him.

They stayed that way for a long time, minutes, maybe close to an hour, until his grip on her loosened.

She shoved back the covers, went to the bathroom, and freshened up. Coming back into the bedroom, she noticed the necklace gleaming on the floor in the firelight. It must've fallen from her pocket when Tak was peeling off her clothes and tossing them wherever.

Kimi threw on clothes and picked up the necklace. "Let's see what's on the flash drive." She sat at the table.

"Better be good considering I took a bullet for us to get it." After he half dressed from the waist down, he joined her and removed the plastic wrap from the food.

She plugged the Type-C flash drive into the phone and accessed it. "There's one document. Named 'Worst-Case Scenario.'"

"I'd say this is it." He ate a spoonful of chili. "Wow. This is really good, even at room temp."

Clicking on the document, she opened it and let out a sound that was half sigh, half grumble.

"What is it?" he asked.

She turned the phone toward him so he could see the screen. "It's never simple with my father."

"It's just columns of numbers." Taking her cell phone, he studied it. "Not a phone number or coordinates. What the hell is it?"

As soon as she saw the number sets with dashes between the digits, a flood of memories from her childhood came rushing back. "I think it's a code that uses an Ottendorf cypher."

Tak popped open the cider and filled their mugs. "Pretend like I don't know what an Ottendorf cypher is and explain."

"It's a cypher that's a series of numbers used with a known piece of text from a book to hide a message."

"Okay. So, obviously the book is *The Wizard of Oz*. How do we use it to break the code?"

"I'll need pen and paper."

Tak hopped up to get some and Kimi dug out the book from her overnight bag.

"Here we go." He'd found both in the top drawer of the nightstand and handed them to her.

She put the phone on the table and pointed to the first number set: 10-2-4-1. "Each set of digits corresponds to a letter. Ten is the page number." She opened the book, turning to it. "Two is the second line on that page. Four tells us to go the fourth word in the line, and one means the first letter in that word." She jotted down the letter G. "Each column should spell out a word. We just have to get the rest of the letters and put the words together."

While she deciphered the code, she ate her bowl of chili. By the time she was done eating, they had the message.

Glacier Ridge
Timber Trail Bank
Safe Deposit Box

Takoda looked up at her. "We'll go first thing in the morning after the roads are cleared. Glacier Ridge should be about a four-hour drive from here."

She nodded, grateful the necklace and book had led to something concrete. But the thought of what they might find in the safe-deposit box filled her with dread.

Chapter Fifteen

The landscape was so familiar to Kimi as they drove through Glacier Ridge. The mountains, the city, the buildings, the streets, the river. "I feel like I've been here before, but I don't ever remember coming here."

"Maybe you did when you were a kid. The Glacier National Park isn't far from here."

Takoda made a right and US Route 2 turned into 9th Street.

"I think there's an ice cream shop a couple of blocks down."

Sure enough, they passed the Sweet Retreat Creamery, and she got a sinking sensation in her stomach.

Once they reached the Timber Trail Bank, Tak parked and cut the engine. "Call your mom. Find out. I need to check in with the guys and get an update anyway."

A coldness prickled her skin, raising goose bumps. "I don't think I want to know."

Tak squeezed her hand. "But you need to know. Your dad picked this bank for a reason. We need to know what it is."

He was right. Calling her mom to ask wasn't about her feelings, it was about the bigger picture. One they needed clarity on.

She dialed her mom at the same time Tak made his call.

"Kimi?" a groggy voice answered just before the final ring.

"Hi, Mom." She glanced at the time on her phone. Eleven

a.m., which made it eight in Hawaii. Not wicked early. She put the phone back to her ear. "Sorry for waking you."

"Is everything okay? Did you get the necklace?"

Her brain went back to the horrible scene in the snowstorm. Gunfire. Running. The fear. Takoda getting shot. The bullets that tore into her mom's and Davey's cars.

Grimacing, she tipped her head. They didn't need to know right now. It would only cause them both to worry. Who was she kidding? They were going to freak out and then panic, wondering if she was going to be okay.

"There's so much I need to you tell, Mom," Kimi said, "and I promise that I will. But right now, I have to ask you something. It might sound odd, but have we ever been to Glacier Ridge?"

"Glacier Ridge?" There was rustling on the other end of the line, like her mom was moving around, getting out of bed. "Oh yeah, a couple of times when you were little. Your dad took you and Jacy up there. Hiking. Fishing. My goodness, that was so long ago. What made you think of that?"

"Do you remember where we stayed?"

"Oh, um, a cabin in the woods. Right next to the Flathead River where you guys went fishing."

"Was it a rental?"

"No, it was a family cabin. Thomas's aunt owned it. Jean McGregor. She barely ever used the place."

"Please tell me you remember the address."

Her mom laughed. "Of course not. Actually, I don't think I ever knew it. I spent the time at an artist's retreat, painting and doing yoga. Why do you ask? Is everything okay?"

Far from it. "I don't want to keep you. You're probably wishing you had a hot cup of coffee in your hands right now."

"You know me too well."

Kimi shut her eyes, wishing she could spill her guts about

it all. "Go get caffeinated. Enjoy your vacation, Mom. We'll catch up and I'll fill you in on everything soon. I promise. Love you."

"All right. Love you. Bye, sweetie."

Disconnecting, Kimi turned to Tak. He was wrapping up his call, but she tapped him on the arm.

"Hold on, Jackson," Tak said. He put his hand over the mouthpiece. "What is it?"

"My dad used to take us up here, hiking and fishing. We stayed at a family cabin right off the Flathead River. At the time, it was owned by my Great-Aunt Jean McGregor. That's all my mom knows."

His eyes flashed with understanding. "Hey, I need you guys to find an address. ASAP." Tak relayed the details. "On second thought, Chance connected us to a hacker, Orson. He'll be able to find it the fastest. I'll call—" Takoda listened for a moment to whatever Jackson was saying. "Okay. Just let us know as soon as you hear anything back." He hung up. "Chance is there at the scene, too. They're going to reach out to Orson. Take care of payment."

"Why are you talking to Jackson?"

"He's pitching in, helping out. I called Logan, but he couldn't talk now because he's dealing with the forensics team. So he passed his phone to his brother."

"Forensics? Is this about the blood at my dad's house?"

Takoda shook his head. "No, but results did come back from the DCI lab. The blood on the phone we found was from two different people. One sample belonged to your dad. There's a fifty percent DNA match to yours," he said, and her heart sank. "There was no match to the other person in the database."

Whose blood was it? Was her dad hurt? Was he even still alive? "Then what's with forensics?"

"They found Big Billy Burdock. Murdered. One shot to the chest and one to the head. Execution style. Looks like he's been dead more than twenty-four hours. Closer to forty-eight. They won't know for certain until the medical examiner looks at him."

She swallowed to fight back the fear slithering through her. "Maybe I wasn't at the top of our ghost's list of things to do when he got to town. What if killing Burdock was?"

He cupped her face in his hand and the total concern in his eyes pinched something in her chest. She was in danger, but as long as he was with her, so was he. Takoda had this fierce protective streak that touched her and worried her. She knew without a doubt he would die to protect her, but she couldn't ever let it come to that.

"Let's find out what's in the safe-deposit box," he said. "I don't want to sit out here."

They climbed out of the truck. Heading for the bank, she adjusted the body armor vest underneath her sweater. Inside, they found the customer service desk.

"Good morning," a young woman with a sleek ponytail said. "What can I do for you today?

"Hi," Kimi said. "I'd like to access a safe-deposit box."

"I'll need your box number and identification please."

Kimi unzipped her purse and handed over her license.

"Thank you." The young woman clacked away on her keyboard. A moment later, she narrowed her eyes at the screen and then flicked a glance back up at them. "I'm sorry. I need to speak to the bank manager." She spun her chair around, got up, and made a beeline for a middle-aged guy in an office.

"What do you think that's about?" Kimi whispered.

"Did Thomas ever get you to sign any paperwork for the box?"

She shook her head.

The young woman returned. “Mr. Pegg will help you.” She pointed back to the office. “He has your driver’s license.”

Takoda put a hand on her back, and they went to the office.

“Hello, I’m Clive Pegg. Please, shut the door and have a seat,” he said, and they did as he asked. “You’d like to access box 317?”

“Yes. I have the key.”

“This is highly irregular,” Mr. Pegg said. “I know your father, Thomas. We spent summers fishing together in Flathead River when we were younger. Over the years, we’ve seen each other whenever he came up. I met you and your brother once. Gosh, you were a tiny little thing. Younger than my girls.” His gaze wandered, and he smiled as if remembering. “Last month, Thomas came in and asked for a discreet, somewhat, uh, how shall I say it…”

“Irregular,” Tak suggested.

Pegg smiled wider. “Yes, Thomas made a discreet, irregular request. He opened a safe-deposit box. Wanted you to have access. But he told me he couldn’t bring you in and have you complete the necessary paperwork at the time. He asked me if you ever came in with the key to grant you access. I agreed to help him. He gave me a picture of you, to ensure no one could come to the bank impersonating you. Thomas seemed particularly concerned about that. Anyway,” Mr. Pegg said, placing four forms on the desk in front of her, along with a pen, and her driver’s license. “I verified your identity. The picture on your license matches. Just sign the forms.” Leaning forward, he lowered his voice. “For my records. Backdate them for me, if you will, and I hope we can keep this just between us.”

“Of course. When did my father open the box? I’ll use that date.”

“December tenth.”

Nerves made her hand tremble when she picked up the pen. Quickly, she signed and dated the forms, feeling unnerved about the process.

"Thank you. I'll show you to the box." He escorted them out of the office and guided them along the way.

"You mentioned how you and Thomas spent summer's together," Takoda said. "His aunt had a cabin around here. You wouldn't happen to know the address, would you?"

"Had? Mrs. McGregor still does. Thomas used it as his address when he opened the four boxes."

Bulging her eyes in surprise, she slid a furtive glance at Tak and mouthed, *Four?*

"Thomas wanted you to have access to all of them," Mr. Pegg said, "but you'll need the keys."

But they only had one.

"The address?" Tak asked. "Of his aunt's cabin?"

Pegg showed them into a secure back room. "It's 202 Bad Rock Way. Take 9th Street to Glacier Ridge Road. Make a right. Only one way to turn on Bad Rock. Last cabin. Right on the river. I was over on Wildcat Lane, the street just before it." He stepped up to box 317 and inserted his key. "Ms. Wheeler."

Kimi inserted her key, and they unlocked the door.

"Take your time." Mr. Pegg left them in the room, closing the door behind him.

There were boxes of varying dimensions, this one was the largest size. She guessed it was 10x10.

Takoda took it out. "It's heavy." He set the box on the long table and flipped the lid up.

She stared at a breathtaking amount of cash, large bills bundled in neat stacks. "How much do you think is in here?"

"Beats me." He picked up a stack and thumbed through it. "Two hundred grand. Maybe more."

"We should count it."

They started taking the stacks out, lining them on the table. At the bottom of the box, there were three more keys.

"We'll have to get Mr. Pegg to open the other boxes. Do you think it's more money?" she asked.

"We'll need to check and see."

"And if it is? What are we supposed to do with it?"

"Leave it here, for now. No way we're walking out of this bank with any cash, not knowing where it came from, especially with those men after you. This is probably what they're looking for."

Her stomach clenched and a wave of nausea hit her. She tore her gaze from the money and looked up at Takoda. "What has my father gotten us involved in?"

Chapter Sixteen

Almost one million dollars.

By their rough count of the money in the first box combined with what appeared to be a similar amount in the other three boxes, Thomas Wheeler had close to one million dollars in cash stashed away in Glacier Ridge.

What concerned Takoda more was that Thomas hadn't used the money to pay Big Billy Burdock and get the loan shark off his back. Or that money could've helped him stay hidden if he was in fact hunkered down somewhere. Why leave it in the bank for Kimi to find?

And what had happened to Thomas Wheeler?

Snowflakes drifted across the windshield as Takoda followed Clive Pegg's instructions. He made a right, turning down Bad Rock Way.

At the end of the single-lane road, one solitary cabin sat along the riverbank. The snow-covered, frozen landscape was beautiful in a stark yet serene way. In the summertime, with the sound of the rushing river weaving through the mountains, it must have been gorgeous. No car was parked in the driveway, but there was an unattached garage.

If Thomas Wheeler was there, Takoda hoped they didn't find him dead inside the cabin. That was the absolute worst thing that could happen.

Takoda would prefer not to find him at all. Then at least there would still be the possibility he was alive somewhere.

Slowly, he turned off the road, down the driveway, but stopped before getting too close to the cabin. "Let me go inside first and clear it."

If her father was there but not alive, he sure didn't want her to see his corpse in whatever state it might be in. The stuff of nightmares that would haunt her forever.

She leaned back in her seat, her expression smooth, but her eyes hardened. "I'm going with you."

"Kimi, I don't—"

"I know what you're thinking. But I'm a nurse. I've seen dead bodies before," she said matter-of-factly. "Whatever we find inside, I can handle it."

This incredible woman had a backbone of steel. He loved that about her.

Loved everything about her.

"Seeing the dead body of a stranger is different. This is your father," he said, and she looked away from him. "And if those men found him, they might've done things to him to get him to talk." Tak was certain she had never seen anyone who'd been tortured, and he didn't want her to start now.

"I don't think we have to worry about that."

"Why not?"

"The curtain moved. Whoever is inside is alive. I hope it's him, so I can kill him myself for putting me through all this." She grabbed the door handle, but he caught her arm, stopping her from getting out.

"Hold on," he ordered, drawing his gun. "We're not going to do anything rash. We don't know what we're walking into. I go in first and you stay behind me. Got it?"

"Yeah, I understand. But I'm not useless."

"I'd never think that."

"When we were at my mom's house, you were worried something might happen, but you didn't give me a chance to help you."

"Help me how?"

"Give me a gun. Like you said, we don't know what we're walking into. If my dad is in there, it doesn't mean he's alone."

And their presence was no longer a surprise.

Takoda hesitated, considering it for only a second, before he bent and withdrew his backup gun from the top of his left boot. He handed her the Ruger LCP Max.

She pressed on the end of the slide around the muzzle with her thumb and forefinger, pulling it back to expose the chamber, making sure the first round was loaded. Released it. Leveled her eyes at him. "I'm good to go."

"I'm impressed."

"Did you really think my brother didn't teach me to shoot and handle myself?"

Of course I did, Jacy whispered in his head.

Takoda grinned. "I should've expected nothing less. Follow me and stay close behind me."

He shouldered out of the pickup. Shut the door with a quiet *snick*. Rounding the truck, he met her on the passenger side. The sheet of snow around the front of the place was pristine and untouched. He wanted to leave it that way. They approached the cabin from around the side.

Staying in the tree line, they swept wide, avoiding the front door and heading instead for the garage. His heart pounded in his ears, but through that dull sound, snow crunched beneath their footsteps. Coming to the unattached garage, he peeked through the transom window at the top of the door.

One vehicle parked inside. Not a two-door Ford Bronco. A red Jeep Wrangler.

Going around the side of the house, they moved in silence. The river came into sight, frozen from the subzero temperatures of the snowstorm. Right before they reached a window, he raised his fist, signaling her to hold. The curtains were open. He peered inside. The shadow of a person moved across the living room to the other side of the house, toward the front door.

Kimi's breath crystallized the air beside him.

He gestured with his head for them to continue around back, where they found footprints in the snow. A pile of chopped wood covered with a tarp. They eased up to the back door. He tried the knob. Locked.

Crouching on the balls of his feet, he slipped his lock-picking tools out of his pocket and got to work on the pin tumbler. Kicking the door in would've been faster, but he didn't want to draw gunfire to their position. Quickly, he popped the door open. They crept inside, and he shut it closed. With Kimi right behind him, they both swept through the mudroom to the kitchen, their guns up, at the ready.

The house was warm and full of golden light. They treaded lightly through the kitchen, which was empty. The smell of food permeated the air. No signs of violence. He stopped behind a wall, his shoulder pressed against the casing of the hallway.

Footsteps shuffled. Whispering in the next room.

Takoda peeked around the casing.

"There!" a woman called out.

The double barrel of a shotgun swung in his direction. Takoda scrambled to the side, sliding Kimi out of the way along with himself just in time.

A massive boom tore into the air, blasting out a window.

Chapter Seventeen

A cry stuck in Kimi's throat as adrenaline rushed through her veins.

The shotgun pumped.

Throwing an arm out in front of her, Takoda held her in place. "Thomas! Stop!"

Was her father there? Was he the one shooting?

Another shot shook the walls, blasting a gaping hole in the Sheetrock next to Tak's head, and a scream escaped her. That had been so close. Inches from hitting him.

She swallowed hard, fighting back the fear clawing through her.

"It's Takoda Yazzie! I'm with Kimi."

Silence.

"We're alone. Put the gun down. We're going to come out." Takoda shifted toward the hole and Kimi grabbed his arm, yanking him back from harm's way.

WHAT IF HER DAD wasn't in his right mind? He could panic. Pull the trigger out of fear. A knee-jerk reaction that could kill Takoda.

"It's all right," Tak whispered to her. He glanced through the hole. "No more shooting. Okay?"

Then Takoda eased into the hall with his gun down at his

side. He beckoned to her to join him. Drawing a deep breath, Kimi stepped out and faced the living room.

Her father stood near the front door, wearing a baggy black sweater and jeans, with a shotgun shaking in his arms. A woman with glasses, stringy blond hair framing her face in a bob, cowered behind him. Slowly, he lowered the barrel toward the floor.

"Dad?" Her heart swelled. No matter the situation, no matter the past grievances, seeing him filled her with an inexplicable sense of hope.

"What…what are you doing here?"

She ran to him and threw her arms around him in a hug. "Thank God. You're alive."

At first, he didn't touch her, then one arm closed around her in a tentative embrace that reminded her of the distance between them. The lack of affection and warmth.

The secrets.

"How did you find me?" Dad asked.

"We followed the clues you left until we ended up at the Timber Trail bank in Glacier Ridge." Kimi let him go, glancing at Takoda when he stepped deeper into the room and up beside her. "The town seemed so familiar, like I must've been here before, and then Mom confirmed it. Clive Pegg gave us the address."

Dad gaped at them, his jaw trembling, as if he was processing their presence. His blue eyes were wide, his hair longer than usual and unkempt, his frame leaner. At seventy-two, he was vibrant and healthy, with a youthful energy the last time she'd seen him. But the man in front of her looked frail and weary, his hair more gray than brown now, as though he had aged a decade in mere weeks. Setting the shotgun down, he rested the barrel against the coffee table beside his leather-bound notebook. That was when she noticed his right hand was bandaged.

The woman behind him appeared to be in her late forties, maybe early fifties. She was wringing her hands, her features taut with terror and uncertainty. It wasn't until the woman's panicked stare landed on the gun in her hand that Kimi realized she was still holding it.

Kimi slipped the weapon into her coat pocket and that seemed to reduce the fear on the woman's face.

"I—I didn't think you would remember this place," Dad said. "You were so little the last time I brought you and your brother." He shoved a shaky hand through his hair. "But you shouldn't have come here. It isn't safe. We just need to buy ourselves a little more time. A few days. Just until next week. Tuesday. Maybe Wednesday."

A prickly tangle of emotions churned within Kimi as she rocked back on her heels. "Shouldn't have come? After everything you put me through, that's what you have to say?"

"What are you talking about?" Dad asked. "Did something happen?"

"A lot happened! There are men after me."

Worry etched into her father's expression as he pivoted toward Takoda. "I hired you to look after her. Protect her. Make sure nothing happens."

"Dad! Don't put any of this on Takoda. I'm alive because of him, after you put me in danger." Stiffening, she beat back the burn of tears suddenly stinging her eyes. "What is going on? And who is this?" Kimi waved a hand at the woman.

"This is Wendy Johnson." Her dad put a hand on her arm, urging her forward.

"Your girlfriend?" Kimi asked.

"No." Wendy shook her head. "We're colleagues. We work together at CCMC."

"Thomas, you owe us some answers." Takoda's tone was far gentler than hers. "Since you took off, Kimi has been followed, mugged, her house broken into, and we were shot at yesterday."

Wendy gasped. "Oh, no."

"Takoda took a bullet protecting me," Kimi said.

His face fell and he bowed his head, but her father didn't respond. This was how their conversations went. He shut down the second it veered into territory that was messy or serious or difficult. What they needed to discuss now was all the above.

"We found the money in the four safe-deposit boxes." Takoda's tone was soft and firm at the same time. "What are you wrapped up in? Does it have something to do with the loan shark, Burdock?"

Dad nodded. "Billy is involved, yes."

"Do you owe him money?" Takoda asked. "We were told you have a lot of debt and needed to pay him off."

Her dad's gaze snapped up, his expression confused, shocked. "Owed him money? I'm not in any debt."

"You should tell them," Wendy said. "They've come this far."

"But they shouldn't be here at all." Dad turned to her. "I left you the money just in case you needed it. A worst-case scenario. I don't want to drag you into this any deeper. This is serious business with dangerous people."

"Burdock is dead," Takoda said flatly. "He was found murdered."

Wendy staggered like she might faint. "We're out of time." Trembling, the woman wrapped her arms around herself. "They're going to kill us next," she said, her voice cracking with a sob.

"No, no, no." Her dad put his face in his hands. When he

looked back up, he was ashen. Shaking his head, he clutched Kimi's shoulders and urged her toward the door. "You have to go. Please. You can't be near me. It isn't safe for you."

"You're unbelievable." Kimi wrestled her arms from his grip. "No place is safe for me *because* of you. We're not going anywhere until we get answers. If you want us to leave, then start talking."

Her dad sighed. "This is so much bigger, uglier, than I first realized. I don't know where to begin."

Takoda put a hand on her father's shoulder. "If this isn't about you being in debt, what is it about?"

Wendy dropped down onto the sofa. "Money laundering."

Kimi flickered a shocked glance at Takoda. By the look on his face, neither of them had expected that one.

"About eighteen months ago," her father said, "the projections of palladium from previous target sites started increasing. Slowly. But steadily until they were much higher than I ever estimated. I spoke to the director of operations about it. Unable to answer my questions, he referred me to Nick Nason, the CFO. Nick pushed me off for months." Dad sat at a small table on the side of the room. "Then one day he came clean with me, or at least I thought he did."

Pulling out a chair, Kimi took a seat opposite him. "Clean about what?"

"He told me the company was in financial trouble. Prices of palladium had fallen. They were in a lot of debt and, to cover it, they had started siphoning money from the pension fund. But Nason had a plan to get everything on track. Erase the debt. Restore the retirement fund. It was all predicated on taking the company public right before the congressional bill is signed. A wave of retail investment would make CCMC whole. But he needed to make the books look financially solid. At the time, he didn't get into the specifics. If I didn't go along with it, he told me the company would face bankruptcy, mass layoffs would happen, jobs and pensions would be lost."

"So, you agreed to go along with it," Takoda said.

He nodded, and Kimi reached over the table, taking his hand in hers. His face softened with surprise. They weren't the hand-holding type, but he just looked so beaten down, so lost. Regardless of their issues, he was a good man with a good heart.

"No one was going to get hurt with Nason's plan," Thomas said. "In fact, it would help people. Then Nick coerced me to start meeting Burdock, way out in the middle of nowhere, to do pickups and bring bags of money back to the company. Insisted it was an essential part of the plan. Not long after that, the numbers in the quarterly reports started climbing. Way off. Too high. And not just for projected palladium, but for revenue."

"What did you do?" Kimi asked.

"I confronted Nason. He yelled at me to keep my mouth shut, my head down, and go along with the plan. Otherwise, thousands would lose their jobs if CCMC filed for bankruptcy. But it felt wrong. *Dirty.* I demanded to know the truth. And he told me."

Dad pulled away from her and propped his elbows on the table, dropping his head in his hands. "About laundering money for a drug cartel. That Burdock made the introduction to the Estrada cartel. How their cut of blood money bolstered the company, and they were hiding it with inflated palladium projections. But he needed me to find a new target area, rich in palladium, before the IPO, to solidify the financials. The board and top shareholders wanted independent verification of minerals at the new target area. They must've gotten suspicious of the inflated numbers. Once I knew the cartel was involved, I refused to cooperate."

Kimi touched his arm. "Did he threaten you?"

"Nason told me about an offshore account he opened in my name. That he'd been funneling money into it to make it look like I'd been taking cartel money on the side. To frame me as a bigger accomplice in all this. He thought he could strong-arm me into finding more palladium for them. But I said *no*. Nason went so far as to have Burdock threaten to assault me at work. Still, I refused."

The video Nason had given them. Everything the CFO had told them had been designed to mislead.

"Is the cash in the bank drug money?" Takoda asked.

"Since the offshore account was in my name, I cleaned it out, but didn't know what to do with it."

Takoda stepped closer to the table. "If CCMC is going public with shady financials, then others in the company must know."

"Of course," Dad said, nodding. "The COO and CEO."

"Is that why you made your resignation so public at the holiday party?" Takoda asked.

"It stopped them from coming after me immediately and directly," he said, "though, I think Nason was the only one among the higher-ups who knew the details about the cartel's involvement."

"They know there's a significant amount of money coming in from somewhere." Wendy leaned forward, putting her arms on her thighs. "I overhead Jeff Randolph, the CEO, mention something about plausible deniability to Nason. The less they know, the better in case things ever hit the proverbial fan. Once the company goes public, there's a lot of money to be made, especially after Randolph gets his cousin to push through the bill banning the import of palladium from Russia."

Kimi had read about how Senator Yates was a staunch supporter of American mines and protecting Montana jobs, but not once had she seen one word about him having a personal connection to CCMC. "Senator Yates and Randolph are cousins?" she asked.

"Twice removed, but yes," Dad said. "CCMC needs one more mine with verifiable minerals. And fast. That's why they're so eager to get their hands on my notebook. They must think you have it." He looked at Kimi. "Or hope that you do."

Takoda scrubbed a hand over his jaw. "Nason needs the book. Not Burdock. So why would a loan shark set up shell companies to hide the fact he hired private contractors to go after Kimi?"

"Shell companies?" Wendy stood and slipped her hands in her pockets. "That sounds like Nason's MO to me. If he could forge documents and open an offshore account in Thomas's name, surely he could do the same with shell companies in Burdock's name. It would keep Nason's hands clean if the paper trail led to someone else."

Dad sighed. "The hole I was in with Nason kept getting bigger and darker. I didn't know what to do. Then the FBI approached me." He reached into his back pocket and pulled out a business card. "Special Agent Kirk Kehoe" was written on the front. "I thought that was the way out. Kehoe persuaded me to learn as much as I could about the cartel, how much money was being laundered, to enlist someone in the finance department to help me get account numbers and stuff."

Kimi looked at Wendy Johnson. "So, you went to her."

Wendy nodded. "Thomas dragged me into this. But it sounded noble. Stopping illicit activity. Crippling a money laundering arm of a drug cartel. Getting CCMC back on the path of the straight and narrow."

"That's how Kehoe sold it to me." Dad glanced up. "But he waited until Wendy and I were in so deep, knowing way, way too much, before he started talking about us testifying and the need to go into the witness protection program. He didn't mention one word about any of that when he first approached me."

"They never do," Takoda said. "It would've scared you off. Made you reconsider."

"Darn right, it would've." Dad slapped a hand down on the table. "We want to sever the connection between CCMC and this drug lord. We want to hurt the Estrada cartel. But the price is too high doing it the FBI's way."

"If I leave," Wendy said, "I don't know what'll happen to my property. That land has been in my family for generations. I don't have kids, but the land means everything to me."

"I won't become someone else." Dad raked his hair back with a hand. "Change my name. Give up my life. Give up the people I love. The work I've devoted my life to." He shook his head. "I won't do it."

Kimi sighed. "You won't continue to work for Nason and the cartel. You won't finish what you started with the FBI. What's your plan?"

"To be free." Her father stared at her, his eyes gleaming with familiar grit and determination. "With Nason, it's all lies. They still laid off hundreds of people. Even if the IPO and new retail investment was enough to save CCMC, there's no walking away from the cartel. Nason made a deal with the devil. Once you're in, you're in until you die. It's impossible to salvage CCMC, the jobs, the pensions, without continuing to wash the cartel's blood money. And with the FBI, it's a different kind of manipulation that makes you sacrifice everything in the end. So, Wendy and I decided to knock down the entire house of cards."

Takoda glanced between Thomas and Wendy. "But how?"

"We made copies of the real quarterly reports," Wendy said, "evidence of the company's actual financial status, and Thomas's true technical readings of the amount of palladium in the mines and sent everything to the shareholders."

Kimi shook her head. "I don't understand. How will that help?"

"The shareholders will demand an audit by an independent third party," Dad said. "The IPO won't happen next week. It'll be an unstoppable domino effect that'll bring CCMC down. With the company bankrupt, they won't be able to launder any more money and Nason won't need me or my notebook. It's the only way to be free of the cartel and the FBI. In my contract with the Stracke Group, I negotiated a position for Wendy and stipulated a clause that they try and fill their upcoming positions with current or former CCMC employees. I didn't tell them CCMC was going to go under. They couldn't guarantee the last part, but they agreed to try to offer them jobs. Wendy and I just needed to ride it out, stay in hiding until enough dominoes fell."

Though fearing for his own life, her father had done everything he could to help innocent CCMC workers. To give them a chance at continued employment and a fresh start with the Stracke Group.

"But why give me the necklace, the book cipher, the key, Dad?" Why involve her in this at all?

"Because you're the only one…who could figure it out."

"The coded message?" she asked.

Frowning, Dad brushed his knuckles across her cheek, a show of emotion so out of character, Kimi was taken aback. "All of it. I even hid a phone in my house that had mine and

Wendy's blood on it. If anything happened to me, to us, I needed someone to know. To piece it together. No matter how big the puzzle is, Kimi, you could always solve it. Even if you were angry at me, disappointed in me, hurt by the wrong thing I said, you never could resist a puzzle."

Unfortunately, that was true.

Takoda stilled, his head tilting like he'd heard something.

"What is it?" Kimi asked him, goose bumps erupting on her skin.

"I'm not sure." Rubbing the back of his neck, he hurried to one of the front windows and peeked out the curtain. "There are fresh tracks in the snow. Someone's here," Takoda said, and a coldness slipped through Kimi's veins.

"Oh, no." Wendy pressed her hands to her chest. "They found us."

Kimi and her father stood as a faint buzzing whirred.

Takoda swore. "Drone." The grimness of his tone sent a shiver down her spine. Hurrying from the window with his gun drawn, he made a beeline for her. "We've got to leave."

Someone kicked in the front door.

"Get down!" Takoda was in action as the words left him, jumping in front of her and shoving her down.

Then bullets shattered the windowpane.

Chapter Eighteen

Foley swept inside the cabin, shooting.

As Takoda returned fire, he made sure Kimi and Thomas were down.

Bullets sliced through the air, puncturing drywall. A round slammed into Wendy Johnson, spinning the woman 180 degrees. The second slug hit her in the back. Her eyes rolled into the back of her head. She swayed and toppled forward.

Takoda dropped to his knee and fired low, catching Foley in the gut and shin. A guttural cry left the man as he fell.

Out the corner of Tak's eye, he saw Kimi and her dad crawling under the table.

Taking aim, Takoda shot Foley in the wrist before the man could squeeze off another round. The Glock hit the floor, and Foley screamed out in agony.

Takoda rushed toward the door, staying low, and kicked it shut. "Go hide in one of the bedrooms and stay there," he said to Kimi.

She clutched her father's arms and brought him to his feet. Thomas's gaze fell to Wendy, his features twisted in anguish, and a sob escaped his mouth. While Kimi dragged her father away from the dead body and into a bedroom, Takoda turned his attention to Foley.

He snatched the lamp from the end table and used his fixed blade to slice the cord. Foley was writhing and swearing. The blood on the floor from his gut was nearly black. The bullet had hit the liver. Foley didn't have long to live. Tak flipped him over onto his stomach, drove a knee into the guy's back, and tied his wrists behind him, eliciting another cry of pain. While the man was still breathing, Tak wasn't giving him a chance to take another shot.

"How did you find us?" Tak asked, and when Foley didn't immediately answer, he pressed his knee into his back again.

"Stop! I'll tell you," Foley said, and Tak eased off him. "A tracker on your truck. The other guy put it there. The one with tattoos. Told us where to find you."

"Who is he?"

"I don't know."

Tak refocused. At any minute, Higgins would try to breach the cabin. The only surprising thing was that it hadn't happened yet. Takoda ran in crouched position, heading toward the back door.

Scrambling into the kitchen, Tak knelt, his back pressed to a lower cabinet. He pulled a smoke grenade from his pocket. After the ambush at Spokane, he was better prepared.

The most likely spot for Higgins to enter was through the back door. A classic tactic for the enemy to cut off all points of escape and close in.

Tak had a view of each door, front and rear, including the one to the bedroom, where Kimi and her father were hiding. Ready to pop smoke and open fire, he stilled.

The air had grown quiet. No buzzing from the drone. No sound of footsteps through the snow.

Silence. Just the steady beat of his heart in his ears.

Had they given up and left? Was it over?

One thought slid through his mind as cold fear slid through his veins. The back bedroom was situated in the corner of the house, with windows on two different sides.

Tak sprang to his feet. Another wave of adrenaline surged through him, propelling him as fast as he could go to the other side of the house.

Racing to the bedroom, he flung the door open.

A gunshot rang out. The bullet ripped into Thomas's abdomen, and her father doubled over.

"No!" Kimi screamed.

Higgins was at the riverside window, gun in his hand, and Takoda lined up his sights.

Another shot split the air.

But Tak hadn't pulled the trigger yet.

Higgins made a gurgling noise, clutched at the bloody wound in his throat, and fell backward with a thud into the snow.

Kimi stood, the gun shaking in her grip.

Takoda hurried into the room.

Thomas was holding his abdomen. His lips were moving, but no words came out of him, like all the air had rushed from his lungs.

Dropping the gun, Kimi ran to her father's side.

A red laser dot popped up on Kimi's chest and danced. A high-powered guidance laser from a weapon.

Tak lunged, grabbing Kimi.

A gunshot whispered overhead. Shattered glass from the west-side window sprayed across the room.

Pain bloomed in Tak's elbow as they hit the hardwood floor. He rolled, covering her with his body, protecting her head with his arm. A sharp exhale rushed from her lips across his face.

Thomas clutched his chest with his other hand and collapsed right before a second shot whispered through the room.

The shooter was using a sound-suppressed sniper rifle. The ghost was still out there.

"Dad?" Kimi's voice was shrill.

The air was quiet. No more shots were fired.

"Stay here. Don't move," Takoda ordered.

Crawling on the floor, he yanked the bottom of the curtains, closing them on the riverside window, which was nearest. Then he crept across broken glass to the west window and did the same thing, obscuring the shooter's visual of the room.

Leaping to his feet, he picked shards from his palms and brushed glass from his pants.

Kimi scrambled to her father. "Tak, give me your knife!"

Unsheathing it, he handed it to her. She sliced through her father's sweater, and beneath it he wore body armor. *Kimi's body armor.* A bullet had lodged in the chest.

Panic gripped his heart. "You gave him your vest?" She must've removed it and got her father to put it on right after the two of them had run into the bedroom to hide. Kimi was a quick thinker, especially under fire. Though Takoda would've preferred it if she had kept the vest on rather than putting her life at risk, even to protect her father.

"I thought he was in more danger than me. I was right."

Blood trickled from the top of the vest across Thomas's neck.

Tak unstrapped the vest and removed it.

Kimi gasped at the sight of the blood leaking from the wound. "The armor was supposed to protect him!"

The vest stopped the bullet Higgins had fired, only knocking the wind out of Thomas. But this… "Rifle rounds are different." Level IIIA armor would slow down the slug, but it'd still penetrate the vest.

Thomas raised a bloody hand and cupped her face. "I'm sorry. I failed you. As a f-f-father. You. Jacy."

"No, Daddy." Tears fell from her eyes. "You didn't."

"Made s-so many mistakes. Forgive me. Please."

Kimi stared at the wound. "Nothing to forgive."

"Go…go. Bigfork. I love you. Always."

"We've got to stop the bleeding," Kimi said, her frantic gaze flying to Tak. "We need the med kit."

The sniper could still be out there. But every second Tak delayed meant another second of unchecked bleeding for Thomas.

He had two smoke grenades and could use them for cover.

"Okay." He picked up the Ruger and shoved it into her hand. "Just in case. I'll be right back." Tak ran to the front door.

Pulling the pin, he tossed the first grenade outside. A thick cloud of white erupted. He darted from the cabin and sprinted through the snow. No potshots taken. Yanking the next pin, he chucked the grenade. Another white cloud bloomed, obscuring him.

He made it to the truck. Snatched the med kit. Bolted back to the cabin without the sniper firing a single round. Takoda hoped it was a sign the ghost had cleared out after shooting Thomas.

In the bedroom, Kimi had her hand over the wound, applying pressure.

Thomas was still, his eyes closed, his head had lolled to the side.

Oh, no. Was he too late?

Tears spilled from Kimi's eyes. "Daddy!"

SEATED AT THE KITCHEN TABLE, Kimi was quiet, her brain in a fog. The house was abuzz with activity, sheriff's deputies swarming everywhere.

A protective sheet covered Wendy's and Foley's dead bodies in the living room. And she was responsible for killing the man outside. She'd pulled the trigger to save her father and herself, but it still wasn't enough because there had been a sniper.

The thought of her father made her heart hurt.

She'd finally connected with her dad—gotten real answers, affection, a heartfelt apology, all the things she'd yearned for from him—only to watch him get shot.

No more tears came. Her eyes were swollen and ached from crying. She was numb. Her limbs were heavy, like her veins were full of lead.

Takoda had cleaned her face and hands. Held her. Let her cry at the unfairness of it all.

Kimi's phone chimed. A text message. She took her phone from her pocket, but she felt disconnected. Like she was having an out-of-body experience.

Looking at the screen, she didn't recognize the number. She tapped on the message and read it.

This is Izzy. The missing person's report was filed by your father's son. Your half brother, Michael. He knew something was wrong when your dad missed his sixteenth birthday.

Takoda cupped her face and wiped her cheeks. She touched her eyes and her fingers came away wet. Tears. She was crying again and didn't even realize it.

"What is it?" he whispered.

She showed him her phone.

He read the text and set her cell on the table. Crouched in front of her. Held her hands. Pressed his forehead to hers.

More tears fell and he wiped them away.

Takoda didn't say anything. What could he say that would take away her pain or answer her new questions or help her to understand this newest bombshell secret? Tak gave her what she needed instead, his support and his comfort.

A deputy handed Takoda a blanket and he wrapped it around her shoulders.

The same deputy turned to the sheriff. "Have we gotten their statements yet?"

"No, and we're not going to," the sheriff said, his narrowed gaze sliding over Kimi and Tak. "We were ordered not to question them."

"Who has the authority to give you that order?"

The telltale *thwump*, *thwump*, *thwump* of a helicopter cut through Kimi's daze, drawing her attention, along with everyone else's, outside the kitchen window. Kimi hoped that she and Takoda had made the right decision.

"You're about to meet him," the sheriff said.

The sleek black helicopter touched down on the expansive field of snow on the side of the house. The door slid open. A man wearing a blazer with FBI stenciled across the front in yellow letters climbed out. Jackson Powell hopped out next.

Kimi looked up at Tak.

"I don't know why Jackson is here," he said, answering her unspoken question.

They had found the card for the FBI agent who had tried to force her father to testify and then go into witness protection. Kirk Kehoe was the only person they knew who might be able to help fix this. So, she called him.

The FBI agent strode into the back door, through the mudroom, into the kitchen. Even if he didn't have on a jacket announcing who he was, he had an air of authority that immediately commanded attention.

Holding a folder in one hand, the agent went up to the sheriff and offered his other hand. "Special Agent Kirk Kehoe. Thank you for securing the scene. I trust my requests were respected."

The sheriff handed him something. Her father's leather-bound notebook in an evidence bag. "They were," the sheriff said. "We reported four dead bodies, instead of the three we've got, like you asked, and didn't question these two. Mind explaining?"

"I do mind. This is my case. End of explanation," Kehoe said simply. "Now, I'll need the room. Excuse us."

The sheriff pursed his lips, eyes narrowing to slits, but he and the deputies began to vacate the house.

Jackson came into the room and stood beside the federal agent. His US marshal badge hung prominently from the chain around his neck, and he wore a windbreaker, too, with his agency's name stenciled on it.

Once they were alone, the FBI agent turned to Kimi and Takoda, who remained standing. "I'm Special Agent Kirk Kehoe. We spoke on the phone."

Kimi couldn't treat her father's chest wound. The body armor had slowed the bullet, preventing the slug from going as deep as it otherwise would have. He needed to be medevaced out of there. The FBI agent was the only one they knew who had the power to make it happen quickly without wasting time. When they spoke on the phone, with her frantic over her father's life hanging in the balance, she agreed to honor whatever conditions he would set in exchange for his help.

"Your father is in stable condition under a false identity. The sheriff's department is going to report that Thomas Wheeler was found dead on the scene here. I believe you both already know Jackson. He's a deputy US marshal assigned to my special joint task force, called Operation Big Sky Guardian. Our job is to bring down the Estrada cartel. Stop their drug smuggling, human trafficking and money laundering in this country by disrupting their supply chains and networks. Our focus is their base of operation in Canada, which uses Montana as their entry point and distribution hub."

"Are you the reason Chief Ed Macon made Detective Logan Powell drop this case?" Takoda asked.

The special agent nodded. "Yes, I am."

Takoda pivoted to Jackson. "When you came to dinner the other night, you were working. You were there as a marshal." Statements. Not questions.

"I was also there as a friend," Jackson said.

"Did he…?" Her voice was hoarse, her mouth bone-dry. Kimi swallowed and cleared her throat. "Did Agent Kehoe send you to Bitterroot Falls the other night? Did he ask you to see if I knew where my father was?"

Sighing, Jackson lowered his head. "Yes, he did."

Kehoe eased forward in front of Jackson. "You're aware your father was working for us?"

"I'm aware you baited my father with promises of getting him out of a bad situation, only for him and Wendy Johnson to later learn you wanted them to testify and go into witness protection. To upend their lives and take them away from everyone and everything they've ever known."

"I never lied to your father."

"You misled him. Same as Nason. To get what you wanted."

"Nick Nason and I are nothing alike," Kehoe said. "He doesn't care about this country, or the people he hurts, or if the money that pays for his lavish lifestyle comes from a cartel that kills tens of millions of people with drugs. Not to mention the human trafficking. Trust me, you don't want me to go into the ugly details of that sordid business."

"Look at me." Takoda stepped up to the agent. "I suggest you change your tone and back off or this conversation is finished."

"I've done you a big favor," Kehoe said. "*Huge.* So, this isn't over until I say it is."

"This is important," Jackson said. "We have a serious problem. Lives are at stake."

"She had to watch as Wendy Johnson was murdered, and her father almost died in her arms. She was nearly killed!" Takoda pointed a finger at Jackson. "Don't tell either of us what's at stake."

"My apologies for getting off on the wrong foot." Agent Kehoe sat next to her at the table. "What you've been through is awful. I'm sorry you've had to experience any of it." The smooth-talking agent looked at Takoda. "Please, sit," he said, gesturing to a chair.

Takoda shook his head once. "I'm good."

"Suit yourself," Kehoe said. "Your father promised to help us get Nason, and Ms. Johnson was supposed to provide financial information regarding the cartel. Account numbers that we could track and monitor to see how Estrada moves their money. We still need that information."

"My father won't testify. He won't go into witness protection."

"I understand," Kehoe said. "But I also told you over the phone that my help, protecting your father, comes at a price."

"What do you want?" Takoda asked, his voice like cold steel.

"I want Ms. Wheeler to contact Nason. Offer him the notebook." Kehoe set her dad's book on the table. "When you meet, get him talking. We need him to incriminate himself. Get him to boast about the cartel, but more importantly, about taking CCMC public. If we can establish intent, we can charge him with a multimillion-dollar pre-IPO fraud scheme. Then we can use the charge as leverage. Get him to flip on the cartel and provide us with all the information Wendy Johnson was supposed to give us."

Kimi shook her head. "You have to be kidding. First, you

put my father in this position that nearly got him killed. Now you expect *me* to help you?"

"Let's get something crystal-clear, Ms. Wheeler. Nick Nason put your father in this position. Pressured him. Coerced him. Used him. Nason got him entangled with the Estrada cartel. And Nason got him shot. He may as well have pulled the trigger and put the bullet in your father himself. I offered Thomas protection. A way out of this mess. We're the good guys here, trying our best, risking our lives to bring down the bad guys. Like Nason. Like the man who shot your father. Like the Estrada cartel."

Kimi clutched the blanket against the cold shiver that ran through her. Squeezing her eyes closed, she considered it. "I don't know." Her father was alive, fighting for his life. She just wanted to focus on him recovering.

"I'm the only thing standing between your father and the next bullet that will kill him," Kehoe said. "As far as the world is concerned, he's dead. We can keep it that way. Once he's released from the hospital, I can have him moved to a DCI safe house here in Montana. Where he'll stay until we eliminate the threats to him. Then he'll be free and clear. But that puts you on the hook to deliver for me."

She looked around the room. "I need time to think about it."

"There is no time," Jackson said.

Kehoe nodded. "He's right. If you're going to help us, it has to be done today."

"Whoa." Takoda raised his palm. "Why today? What's the rush?"

"It was a good thing Jackson went to dinner the other night." Kehoe's hard gaze swung between Kimi and Takoda. "He got a look at the guy at the bar. Passed us the pictures you pulled from the surveillance cameras."

Takoda frowned. "But the pictures were lousy. Grainy. You couldn't see the guy's face, and a hacker we hired couldn't identify him."

"Your hacker didn't need to because I already know who he is." Kehoe put the folder on the table, opened it and took out a clear picture of the ghost's face. "His name is Alvaro Aguilar. He's the top hitman for the Estrada cartel. They don't dispatch him to collect money or fetch notebooks." Kehoe tapped her dad's brown-leather book. "When they unleash this monster, it's only for one purpose. He's cleaning up loose ends. Burdock. Your father. Wendy Johnson. If he finds out Thomas is still alive, he will come back to finish the job." The agent paused, letting that sink in. "We're aware your father set certain things in motion to stop the IPO of CCMC. The news is going to break any day. When it does, the impending bankruptcy of CCMC will be announced. Then the Estrada cartel won't have any need for Nason. He's a dead man walking unless we can flip him first and get him to agree to testify against the cartel. Time is of the essence."

Kimi took it all in and one thing struck her as a red flag. "Wait a minute, how would the cartel know that there are loose ends? That my father, Wendy or Burdock could be a threat to them. I mean, isn't it business as usual for them? Why is this Aguilar even here?"

"After your father jumped ship from CCMC and went to work for the Stracke Group, there was no movement on the part of the cartel. I thought we could still pull this off, bring Mr. Wheeler and Ms. Johnson around to see our perspective. It wasn't until your father and Ms. Johnson deviated from the plan by running, which forced me to reveal their identities to the joint task force. So that we could track them down and come up with plan B."

"That's when the cartel took action?" Kimi asked.

The special agent's expression turned grim. "Forty-eight hours after I briefed the task force about your father and Johnson and the need to find them, Aguilar landed in Missoula."

Understanding dawned, and a cold rush prickled beneath her skin. "Are you saying you have a leak in your task force?"

"Yes," Jackson said. "We have to assume the cartel knows the identity of each member of the task force as well as any assets we've discussed in the group."

Not only was her father in danger, so was Jackson.

"Was Thomas's plan to stop the IPO discussed?" Takoda asked.

The agent nodded. "Yes, but Nason is still alive. For now. Today might be our last chance to get to him. Only Jackson is assisting me with this. No one else from the task force, to be on the safe side. And no one from the task force, other than Jackson, will know your father is alive. Help us get the man who ruined your father's life and nearly got him killed."

Kimi took a deep breath. Her father might not want her to work with the FBI, but he and Wendy Johnson would want her to do what she could to stop the cartel. And this was the only way she could protect her father until it was safe for him to go back home. "I'll do it. Under one condition."

"I think I've already gone above and beyond for you and Thomas," Kehoe said. "But what is it?"

"Nason doesn't get full immunity. I know you'll give him a lesser sentence or something." She wasn't naive. "But he doesn't get off scot-free. I want justice."

Agent Kehoe gave her an appraising look, then offered his hand. "You have a deal, Ms. Wheeler."

Kimi looked at Jackson. "Can I trust this man to keep his word?"

"Yes. We are the good guys here. He'll keep his word." The sincerity in Jackson's eyes and voice swayed her.

"Okay." She shook the agent's hand.

Kehoe took out a flip phone, setting it on the table, along with a phone number written on a piece of paper. "Call Nick Nason. Set up a meeting. Tell him you've got your dad's notebook and will give it to him. But you want one hundred thousand dollars in cash and for him to leave you alone. No more being followed. Attacked. Or any further attempts on your life."

"Why ask for the money?" she wondered.

"Nason is filth. If you don't come across as greedy as him, he won't buy it."

Takoda finally sat. "What if he says he needs more time?"

"Then tell him you'll offer the notebook to the Stracke Group. Nine o'clock is the deadline. I guarantee he'll agree to the meet."

"But…" Kimi swallowed. "It'll be a trap, won't it? I mean, for us."

"Yes. Both sides will set traps. We just have to be better than him."

Takoda took her hand and held it. "I'll be with you. Every step of the way."

Nodding, Kimi picked up the phone and made the call to Nason.

Chapter Nineteen

The closed palladium mine came into view. Takoda parked behind two black SUVs. Nason had brought plenty of company. But they hadn't expected him to be alone.

Nick Nason was like a hyena. A vicious scavenger that profited from the work of others and hunted in a pack.

Also, Orson had given them a heads-up. The hacker was painstakingly thorough and had tampered with Red Sentry's system, creating an alert to notify him if any other personnel were assigned to the same contract as Foley and Higgins. Even though Burdock was dead, the shell company allegedly in his name hired four more men today. Marked urgent and high priority. Confirmation that Wendy Johnson had been right about Nason using Burdock to cover his tracks with Red Sentry.

Orson passed along pictures, names and background information on the four new Red Sentry security personnel. Typical credentials; prior military or law enforcement. The one guy they were worried about was Ulysses Oldman. He had a unique designator beside his name, no background information readily available, and was the highest paid man on the contract.

Their best guess was he had Special Forces training. Regardless, the goal was to take extreme caution, protect Kimi, and get out of there unharmed with a confession from Nason.

The only hitch was if Nason talked, then it definitely meant DEFCON 1 and Nason didn't intend for them to leave the mine alive. They'd already suspected as much and had prepared for the worst.

Why else choose the deserted mine as the meeting place? The perfect location to dispose of bodies.

They climbed out of the truck and got their bearings. Tak had brought Eli and Bo as backup. Chance, Winter, Declan and Logan were with Agent Kehoe and Jackson in the chopper, waiting to swoop in and apprehend Nason. Then close in on the mine and come to the rescue if necessary. They just needed the signal.

No security personnel was outside. On the slow drive in, Eli had scouted the surrounding area with a dual-screen, binocular-infrared and night-vision device. Military-grade. Eli had given the all-clear outside.

They each had a pair of dual binoculars as part of the plan.

"Get him talking," Takoda said, coming up beside Kimi. "Play to his ego. For men like him, it's always a weakness."

"How will I know when he's said enough?" she asked.

"We'll tell you," Eli said. "Something you won't mistake. Then we'll try to make a graceful exit."

Kimi unzipped her coat and touched the collar of her sweater, where Kehoe had put the wireless listening device. The higher and more exposed it was positioned, without being detected, the better.

Tak caught her hand. "Don't mess with it."

"I'm trying not to." She took a deep breath. "Nerves."

"Give us a minute," Tak said to the guys, and they gave them a little space. He put her palm on his chest. "Focus on talking. We'll do the rest. Remember, if things kick off, take cover. When there's no cover?"

"Drop."

People would aim for body parts, not the dirt. Though she was armed, he hoped there wouldn't be a need for her to use the weapon again. She'd already killed one man. Kimi was a healer, and the weight of taking a life was heavy on her shoulders, dimming the spark in her eye. If he could spare her from going through that tonight, he would.

"If the plan doesn't work," she said, "if anything happens—"

Leaning down, he cut her off with a kiss.

TAKODA REALLY KISSED HER. All mouth and muscle as he brought his arms around her. Threw his whole body into it. Those lips crossing over hers, deepening the kiss with each pass. His tongue licked against hers, drawing a moan up her throat. His fingers slipped into her hair and he held her close for more until there was a pulsing inside her, around her, as if the air came alive, and her nerves settled, replaced with a familiar hunger that burned through her.

He broke the kiss and stared down into her face. "I'm so in love with you that I'd be lost without you. I won't let anything happen to you."

"The feeling is mutual. I'm not worried about me." She curled her fingers into his sweater, her nails scraping the body armor he wore beneath it. "Don't die in there. Promise me."

It was unfair, unrealistic, to ask him to give his word about something like that when there were so many factors beyond his control. But she needed some reassurance or she wouldn't be able to go through with this.

"I'll do my best for you." He brushed his lips over hers. Another soft, warm kiss. "Let's get this done."

The lock on the main double doors had been cut so they could get in. Lanterns had been placed along the dirt floor for illumination, giving the main entrance an eerie glow. Bo had given them all emergency light sticks that they could activate with a snap.

As a teenager, she had been in a mine once with her father.

She didn't like it then and she didn't like it now.

The musty, stale air was so strong with the hint of mold, she nearly choked. An arching ceiling soared overhead. The rock walls trapped the cold temperatures. A constant chill filled the air, even in the summer. Now, it was freezing, their breaths crystallizing in the air.

Wires ran the length of the wall, connected to small lights that either no longer had power or deliberately hadn't been turned on.

No one went in guns blazing, though, the guys had their weapons drawn at their sides. They were all playing it cool, but she was anything but. Her heart was racing, a dull headache pounding in her temples.

Kimi had a gun just in case. She never imagined—despite the training with her brother that prepared her—she'd have to kill someone one day. Taking a life was no easy thing, even in self-defense, and she had to learn to live with it. But everything was overshadowed by her concern for her father and what she had to do next with Nason. Protecting those she loved was second nature, and she was ready to use the gun or any other means to keep them safe.

Following the glowing lights along a slight curve in the path, taking them deeper so the front doors were no longer visible, they came to an opening, where they found Nick Nason and his four goons standing to one side. Bright lanterns had been set around the space. Two tunnel openings were further back. Beyond one of those, she spotted light reflecting across the surface of a huge pool of water.

An abandoned mining cart sat at the opening of the other tunnel, blocking the entrance. Their footsteps echoed through the damp space as they approached Nason. This entire situation had her on the verge of wanting to jump out of her skin, but she focused on talking.

"Nason, where's the money?" she asked.

One guy tossed a duffel bag at Eli's feet. She couldn't remember his name. The only person Takoda demanded she steer clear of no matter what was Ulysses Oldman. At six-four and two hundred and fifty pounds, he was the biggest guy in the room, making him easy to pick out.

Kneeling, Eli unzipped the bag and pretended to check it. He slipped the strap on his shoulder as part of the ruse, no doubt prepared to drop it at the first sign of trouble.

The meeting spot was tight. Close quarters where rock walls and gunfire didn't mix. Bullets would ricochet. Anyone could be killed. She hoped that meant Nason wanted to avoid a shootout.

"Where's the notebook?" Nason asked.

Kimi took it out of her coat pocket and held it up. The notebook shook in her hand. She tried to stay calm, an impossible task.

"Hand it over," Nason said.

"First, I want to know why you roped my father into your scheme instead of leaving him alone."

"He asked too many questions and started demanding answers."

"You could've stonewalled him. Spun some story. But you didn't. Instead, you deliberately dragged him in deeper. Coerced him to pick up the drug money from Burdock. You made him a target."

Nason shrugged. "Thomas had a big, weeping heart. It was his Achilles' heel. He made it so easy for me to play him. He was willing to keep his mouth shut and do as I told him if he thought he was saving jobs and pensions. The fool that he was didn't even want anything for himself. Why not get him to do the dirty work? The less interaction I had with the Estrada cartel or Burdock, the better for me."

"Did you really believe laundering drug money was going to save the company? Or was it always just about you lining your pockets?"

Nason laughed. "I didn't get the brilliant idea to *save* the company by taking it public with the IPO until Randolph found out what I was doing. He was livid until he saw how lucrative it is to be in business with the cartel."

The guy was a talker, which didn't bode well for them.

She looked around, trying to figure out where to take cover. "Then you realized with the fake financials and the IPO that you could make even more by scamming investors?"

"When Randolph confronted me, I was forced to think quick on my feet. That's how I do some of my best work. I know the ins and outs of what the SEC is looking for when a company has an initial public offering. I know the loopholes. The things they miss. The IPO is just the start. Once the bill is passed in congress, the price of palladium will skyrocket, the company will eventually be made solvent, and then there'll be that much more Estrada money I'll get to pocket." He grinned, looking like a ghoul in the lantern light. "The notebook. Now."

Kimi glanced at Takoda. Did they have enough?

"We're golden," he said with a nod.

Swallowing hard, she tossed the book into the center of the space and shuffled deeper into the room. "The layoffs, the pensions you put at risk, did that mean anything to you?" A part of her needed to know if this man had a heart. A soul.

"Sure, it did. The infusion of cartel money was just on the books. When I had to lay off people anyway, Thomas became a thorn in my side, and I cared very much about that.

The daily irritation I endured at seeing his face, hearing his voice, suffering his complaints and pleas to help the workers. *Ugh*. Grated on my nerves. He had to go." Nason stepped forward and picked up the notebook and thumbed through the pages. "Now that I have this, I have zero regrets he died slightly sooner than anticipated."

All this man cared about was stroking his ego and raking in more cash. He didn't care about anyone except himself. Nason wasn't simply dangerous, maybe he was evil. But he was definitely heartless.

"A hundred grand isn't enough. I should've asked for more," Kimi said, edging closer to the mining cart. "Because of you, my father and Wendy Johnson are dead! Their lives are worth more."

"Shoulda, coulda, woulda." Nason strode toward the exit.

Kimi put her hand up to her mouth, hiding her lips. "He's leaving," she whispered into the mic.

"Thomas and Wendy outlived their usefulness," Nason said. "And so have you." He looked back at his goons "Take care of them and that bag of money is yours."

Then all hell broke loose.

One second everyone held their position, not making any sudden moves. In the next second, everyone shifted. Guys drawing knives and lunging, and chaos ensued.

Kimi kissed the dirt as Jacy would've called it, dropping to the ground and rolling toward the steel cart.

Gunfire erupted. Tak and the other guys went for the lights first, shooting out the lanterns.

Darkness was their friend. The Red Sentry thugs would be blind while Tak, Eli and Bo would be able to see with the dual-screen binoculars.

Bullets pinged and bounced off the walls and the steel

mining cart behind her, each muzzle flash illuminating the free-for-all in the space. Kicking. Punching. Blades slashing.

Water splashed—someone must've fallen into the huge pool in the first tunnel. From the sounds, two men were fighting in the water.

Staying low and flat, she trembled, trying to ignore the churning in her gut and the rippling tension that made her blood run cold at the thought of Takoda or any of their friends getting hurt.

A bullet brought a chunk of the rock wall down near her, and a scream slipped from her lips.

More blows were exchanged in the darkness. Someone was grappling on the ground. An anguished roar echoed through the chamber.

Light flicked on in the tunnel with the pool, an emergency glow stick beaming bright. Another stick illuminated near the exit.

Kimi snapped one of her chem lights and tossed it into the center of the space. Frantically, she looked around. Several of the Red Sentry goons-for-hire were down. Eli was wet, but on his feet. Bo was slowly climbing to his feet, out of breath.

She spotted Tak.

Ulysses surged forward, hiking his shoulder into Takoda's midsection and hefting him off the ground before slamming him into the rock wall. The men grappled and fell to the dirt, rolling and grunting and punching.

Dread curled her stomach. Bo and Eli raised their weapons. But they didn't dare shoot. The movements were too jerky, quick, and Takoda could have just as easily been hit.

Then a gun went off, making her flinch.

For a second, no one moved. No one seemed to breathe. Horror raced through her.

Ulysses was on top of Tak. Both simply lay there. Still. Quiet.

Panic welled inside her. “Takoda.”

But Ulysses moved, and Kimi’s heart stopped. *No.* Ulysses must’ve been the one to shoot. The wrong man survived.

A small cry squeezed from her throat. Anger, pain, fear—all fired through her. She jumped up, needing to get to Takoda, to claw that brute off him. To kill Ulysses with her bare hands.

Bo caught her by the arms, stopping her as Ulysses started to rise like some villain from a horror movie. But then his body was shoved to the side.

His *dead* body.

Takoda sat up with a groan. A rush of overwhelming relief drove Kimi to her knees. He was alive.

A FIERY PAIN bloomed in his abdomen. Takoda pressed his hand to his side, where Ulysses had cut him. His vision blurred, but he saw Kimi clearly when she launched herself at him, throwing her arms around his neck.

“Ouch,” he grunted.

She eased back. “You’re hurt. Let me see.”

He removed his hand

Kimi lifted his sweater. “He stabbed you.”

“More of a slash, really.” Takoda sucked in a sharp breath through the pain. “I don’t think it’s too deep.”

“But you’re wearing body armor.” She applied pressure to the wound.

His chest tightened at the look of worry on her face. “It’s bullet resistant. Not knife resistant.”

She gave him a sad smile and kissed him.

Eli sloshed through the chamber, soaking wet.

Bo put two fingers to his ear. "They got him. Nason is in cuffs as we speak. Winter and Jackson are headed inside."

Mission accomplished. One step closer to stopping the Estrada cartel and getting Thomas back to Bitterroot Falls, living the life he wanted.

Takoda took Kimi's hand and stared in her eyes. "As I was fighting that guy, I realized he was better than me. When I hit the ground and he had the advantage, all I could think about was you. Doing my best, surviving, for you. Kimi, I've been in love with you for a long time. Can't-see-straight, get-ridiculously-jealous-when-you're-with-someone-else kind of love. I want to marry you," he said, and she gaped at him. "But we can wait. I mean, I'll do it right. Make sure you're happy and ready and then I'll pop the question with a big ring. I just know without a doubt that this is right and I needed to tell you."

"Yes!"

"What?"

She kissed him. Leaning in, she kissed him deeper. Pain flared in his gut and he groaned.

"Sorry," she said. "Yes, to all of it. No waiting necessary. But a ring would be nice."

If he could see her smile every day for the rest of his life, he'd be the luckiest man on the planet. "You got it."

You better marry her, Jacy said low, so faint like a whisper in the wind.

The words, his best friend's voice, whether real or imagined, brought him peace.

Peace that Jacy would approve, be happy for them, and wish them well.

It was a good thing, too, because Kimi was it for him. She was his forever.

Chapter Twenty

Kimi wasn't sure how she was going to get through today—her dad's fake memorial service.

Thomas Wheeler was alive and recovering in a hidden location in Montana, one unbeknownst even to her. She hadn't seen him since her dad had been medevaced out of Glacier Ridge. The hardest part was that they couldn't tell anyone the truth. Not friends. Not family. Not even anyone in IPS. Everyone had to believe that Thomas Wheeler was dead.

It was the only way to ensure his safety until the threat with the Estrada cartel was eliminated.

A very real, very deadly, threat. Nick Nason had been taken into custody. Special Agent Kehoe had been smart enough to hold him in a cell and not move him until Nason flipped, giving them all the information they needed. Account numbers. Amounts. Timelines. Details they could use to establish a pattern and track other cartel funds.

As soon as Nason was exposed, in the process of being transferred to a different facility, someone—Alvaro Aguilar—put two bullets in him. One in the chest. One in the head.

The CEO and COO of the Cutthroat Creek Mining Company were charged with the pre-IPO fraud scheme. Kimi was able to give her dad's notebook to the Stracke Group. Hundreds of people were going to be hired by them instead of losing their jobs. Her dad might not have been able to save

CCMC, but he had preserved the livelihood of so many in the town.

Kimi looked over at Takoda sitting behind the wheel of his truck as he parked in the church's lot. The tension inside her released. With him at her side, she could get through anything.

Over the past week, they'd been in his house, sharing one bedroom. Gone was the frustration and denial. No more pushing each other away. No more holding back. He kept telling her how much he loved her. How wrong he'd been for waiting so long to act on his feelings. How right he believed they were together. Takoda wasn't going anywhere. She could count on him to be there for her always. As her husband. One day.

Tak hopped out, crossed the front of the truck and opened her door for her. Taking her hand, he helped her out, shut her door and held her. Pressed his forehead to hers. Stared in her eyes. "Ready?"

He was her rock, and she was going to lean on him now.

"No, but I don't want to be late for his service. Besides, Mom and Davey are already inside." They'd left twenty minutes earlier. "We should go in."

He kissed her, took her hand, and they interlaced their fingers as they walked.

The weather was beautiful. Warm enough to melt the ice on the ground. The sky was a bright blue and cloudless. The breeze was gentle. Her father would be pleased with it.

She also hoped that he approved of her donating the money from the safe-deposit boxes to the American Institute of Professional Geologists to be used for scholarships. Her dad would want some good coming from the money, to help people, especially if it paved the way for there to be more geologists in the world.

They rounded the corner. Kimi stopped. The entire crew was there, waiting outside the church. Chance and Winter.

Summer and Logan. Autumn. Declan. Nora and Bo. Eli. Even Jackson.

"I can't believe you're all here," she said, determined not to cry.

"Of course we came." Summer hugged her. "You lost your dad, and you need us. We're here for each other, through all of it."

"The highs and lows," Chance said. "The good weather and the storms."

Guilt and appreciation swelled in her chest. She wished she could tell them the truth. One day, she hoped they'd understand.

She was lucky to have them.

They all huddled around her and Kimi had never felt such an overwhelming outpour of love and support. This was the true meaning of family.

Kimi and Takoda entered the church. She did her best to get through the greetings and hugs and condolences as they made their way to the front of the nave.

At the second row, she went to join Mom and Davey when the woman seated in the first pew stood, turning to her.

"I'm Lena. You're Kimi, right?"

She swallowed hard. "Yes."

"This is Michael," Lena said, and the young man in a dark suit stood up.

He was so tall for a sixteen-year-old, and it was surprising how much he looked like Jacy when he'd been that age.

"Hi." Kimi offered her hand.

Michael hugged her instead. A tight, genuine embrace that lasted far too long.

"It's nice to finally meet you," she said. "I hate that it's under these circumstances, but I hope we can spend time together and talk." Start building a relationship.

"Me, too. I have so many questions for you and stuff to share."

She bet he did. "It's the same for me."

"Would you sit with us?" Michael asked.

Drawing in a deep breath, Kimi nodded. She squeezed Tak's hand, and he didn't let go. They both went to join Lena and Michael.

Nerves slid through Kimi as she stared at the large photo of her father on the memorial board. She'd pushed off going to the rez, despite his wish, not knowing what to say, how to start the conversation that her father should've initiated. Thankfully, the minister came out, went to the pulpit, and she began the service.

Tak leaned in. "Great timing," he whispered in her ear.

Grinning at how he seemed to read her mind, she couldn't agree more. She loved him so much.

The minister gave a moving sermon and praised her father's good qualities. People shared stories about her dad. Most of them were funny, but all of them highlighted how he was such a passionate and kind man.

"Now, Lena, Thomas's partner, would like to sing a song."

Agent Kehoe had stressed the importance to Kimi for everyone, absolutely everyone, to believe her dad was dead. If they could keep him alive, protected, it would be worth it in the end. She hoped he was right.

Michael reached under the pew and pulled out a guitar. With a smile, Lena took it and stood in front of the nave where someone had set up a microphone for her.

"Thomas loved this song. He loved Montana. He loved the land here," Lena said. Then she sang "Montana Melody" by LeGrande Harvey. Not only was she a skilled guitarist but also had a hypnotic voice.

Montana, Montana, my home.

Everyone clapped once Lena finished.

When she returned to her seat, Kimi turned to her. “That was beautiful. Truly.”

The minister stood at the pulpit. “The family has chosen Kimimela Anne Redbird Wheeler to speak on their behalf.”

Takoda gave her hand another quick squeeze.

Kimi got up and went to the microphone. “Hi. I really wasn’t sure what to say about my dad. Then my mom told me to just speak from the heart. So, here goes. My father was a brilliant geologist. A braver and stronger man than I ever realized. Fearless in his convictions. He was a fighter, determined to live his life on his terms. There are so many things that he taught me and that I learned to love because of him. Hiking. Fishing. All about codes and ciphers. And puzzles. I will work on a puzzle no matter how big or how long it takes. Or how difficult it might be. I definitely inherited his tenacity,” Kimi said, and everyone laughed. “In many ways, my father was an enigma to me. I only wish that I had had more time to figure him out.” She promised herself that when she saw him again, things would be different. She would try harder. “Even though our relationship was strained and distant at times, in the end, I never felt closer to him. Or prouder of him. I love him. He will be greatly missed.”

Once the minister wrapped up the service, everyone stood, preparing to go to the repast in the auxiliary part of the church.

Lena touched her arm. “Can I speak to you for a minute, in private?”

Kimi nodded to Tak that it was all right. Michael stepped over to the side, but he wasn’t alone long. Her mom and Davey went straight over to him.

“I wish we could’ve met before today,” Lena said.

“Dad asked me to go Bigfork. He didn’t get a chance to

tell me why. Then again, I don't know if he ever would've told me. Do you know why he didn't tell me about Michael?"

"That's what I wanted to talk to you about. Your father was hesitant to have a child with me. He was so worried that he'd mess it up. Then one day he said to me, 'Lena, if we can't change, learn from our mistakes, grow and become a better person, what's the point of this journey?' After Michael was born, he told Jacy first. Your brother got very upset."

Kimi imagined the conversation and it was easy to see Jacy exploding.

"He felt like your dad was trying to replace you two. Start over," Lena said. "He told your father that if he loved you, Kimi, then he wouldn't break your heart by telling you about Michael."

That knocked the wind right out of her. But she could see it. "I was fourteen. Hormonal. Confused about so many things. My relationship with Dad was difficult. Fracturing at that point. It would've been a big blow to me. Back then. But not now."

"Thomas didn't know how you'd ever take it, but he believed Jacy knew you better than he did. So, he promised not to tell you. Since I respected that, when Michael filed the missing person's report, I asked Joe Midthunder not to tell you either. He conveyed that it was hard for you, not knowing who filed the report. I'm sorry about that. Your dad loved you, both you and Jacy, so much. Thomas just didn't know how to mend what was broken between you guys."

"It wasn't entirely his responsibility," Kimi admitted. "Not after I became an adult. I should've put in more of an effort. I regret that. But I'm glad we finally connected." She had a chance to forgive him, to accept the love he was able to give. One day, they would get their fresh start.

"Thomas wanted half of his ashes spread on Bitterroot

Mountain and the other half on Bigfork. The weather is supposed to be just as nice tomorrow as it is today. We'd like to do it then. Would you and Aiyana be able to join us? Thomas would've wanted that."

Agent Kehoe assured her the cremated remains were fake, the kind they use in Hollywood. Having a memorial to sell the idea was one thing. Spreading was like a final goodbye.

"Lena, if you don't mind, could we wait? Say, a year?"

Her father should be back home by then. Kehoe thought it would be much sooner since he was activating a deep cover asset within the Estrada cartel. Jackson was hopeful they'd be able to pull off Operation Big Sky Guardian.

Kimi's fingers were crossed.

"I thought getting to it would be better, but we can wait. I'm in no hurry to say goodbye to him." Lena wrapped her in a warm embrace.

Kimi hugged her back. "Is it okay if I speak with Michael?"

His mom waved him over.

"I have something for you." Kimi opened the purse Jacy had given her. It went with every color and every outfit, in her opinion. She took out her dad's signet ring with the Wheeler family crest. "Dad would've wanted you to have it."

Smiling, Michael slipped it on his finger. "His ring."

"It's your ring now."

"Thank you."

Kimi noticed people exiting through the side door that led to the auxiliary building.

"Are you staying for the repast?" Michael asked.

"Yeah, I am."

"Would you sit at our table?"

She nodded. "Sure." It was time she got to know her little

brother. They could exchange numbers and set up a day to spend time together one-on-one.

Lena and Michael headed off through the side door.

Turning around, Kimi found Takoda waiting for her. She slipped her arms around his waist.

He drew her closer. "You did great."

"Think so?"

"I know so. How do you feel about having another brother?"

"Strange. But in a good way. The more family," she said, glancing over at their motley crew, who had shown up for her, who she loved, "the better." She put her head on his chest, soaking in his warmth.

"I was thinking we should take a trip," he said.

Looking up at him, she smiled. "Just the two of us? On a warm, sandy beach?" Where he was going to propose, down on one knee, with a ring.

"You read my mind." He got that soft lovey-dovey look that was just for her. Then he kissed her quick and hard, making her tingle from her scalp to the soles of her feet. "I love you, Kimi. You're perfect. Well, perfect for me. We belong together."

"I was trying to tell you, but you were being stubborn. Next time, listen to me sooner."

"I promise." Grinning, he caressed her face, and his fingers slipped into her hair.

She loved his touch. Craved it. "I'm going to hold you to that, mister."

"I wouldn't have it any other way."

* * * * *

Look for

Big Sky Manhunt

the next thrilling installment of
Juno Rushdan's bestselling Harlequin Intrigue miniseries
Ironside Protection Services

On sale April 2026
Wherever Harlequin Intrigue books and ebooks are sold.

And catch up with the previous titles,

Big Sky Slayer
Big Sky Safe House

Available now!